CHRISTMAS WITH THE COCKROACHES

by
LIBBE LEAH

Cover Art and Inside Illustrations by Kristin Musser

Revised and Edited by Allyson T. Woolf

ISBN: 1624360068
ISBN-13: 978-1-62436-006-0

Reel Culture Press | Los Angeles
www.reelculturepress.com

DEDICATION

In memory of my friends Ruthie, Kristine, Janet, and Bill whose spirits dwell in the characters of this book. To Ruthie, who could never pass by a mirror without looking at herself; to Kristine, the prima donna; to Janet, for her endless sense of humor and big heart. And to Bill, for inspiring this book with his song, "*Christmas with the Cockroaches.*"

You are missed.

CONTENTS

CHRISTMAS WITH THE COCKROACHES

Chapter One

LEAVING MANHATTAN

This will be a great holiday for the Guldstein family, even if they are celebrating it late. It is extra special since they are finally moving out of their apartment in lower Manhattan where the Roach family has been bugging them ever since they were first wed.

One of Gerry and Stephanie's most memorable times was their wedding day. The sky was crystal blue without a cloud, and a tropical breeze gently brushed the cheeks of the guests with pleasant warmth.

Stephanie's ivory gown was simple but elegant. It lay across Gerry's bed ready to be worn in a few hours, after her bridesmaids' arrival to help her with her hair and dress. The limousine then whisked her away to the temple to await her walk down the aisle with her father to the chuppah—the wedding canopy. The ceremony would take place at a synagogue in Manhattan that Gerry's mother and father attended. It was a small building with a hall and lawn in the back for guests to celebrate, perfect for Stephanie who wanted the wedding to be low-key.

There were several out-of-town guests already lolling in the reception hall, and all four in-laws were madly dashing about seeing to last minute details. Stephanie's sister, Gabby, who never traveled to the United States, came from Israel to watch her sister marry, and was perspiring from bearing the brunt of the work that needed to be done before the ceremony.

Gerry nervously paced the floor of his best man's apartment, small beads of sweat dotting his pale forehead. "You have the ring, don't you?" he repeatedly asked his closest friend.

The last few hours somehow passed and everything was ready to go. The rabbi appeared carrying the ketubah, and everyone assembled in their seats to watch as Gerry and Stephanie signed the gold-edged marriage contract, written in calligraphy. The wedding party was lined up prepared to take their turns walking down the aisle, while the guests were craning their necks to catch a glimpse of the beautiful bride.

Everything was proceeding without a hitch until Gerry's Aunt Edith from Tel Aviv clumsily stepped on the hem of her own gown and lurched forward, only able to catch her balance with help from one of Stephanie's school chums who was seated nearby. Stephanie stopped in her tracks, taken by surprise, and tried to maintain the smile on her face.

"Oh dear me!" Aunt Edith bellowed in a sorrowful wail. Soft laughter traveled like a wave throughout the crowd.

Gerry gazed at his wife as she approached the chuppah, where he stood waiting. Although the train of Stephanie's gown was unusually long, she didn't falter as she circled her husband-to-be seven times as gracefully as a swan. Gerry was happy beyond words. They exchanged vows and placed the rings on each other's fingers.

Finally, it was time for Gerry to lift the veil from Stephanie's face to kiss his new wife. He gazed at her, and just as he was about to lift the covering from her face, he hesitated…blinking his eyes to be sure of what he thought he saw on top of Stephanie's veil. There, nestling near her hairline, was a small, dark cockroach. Gerry didn't want to draw anyone's attention to the roach, and certainly not Stephanie's, so he leaned in and kissed her as passionately as he could without setting either one in a frenzy. Little did Steph know…

The rabbi saw it and dropped his prayer book, shouting "Oy!" That startled Stephanie and she was puzzled by his outburst. The family seated in the front row witnessed what had happened and were coughing and whispering. Even though their peaceful wedding had been disrupted, they carried on with the ceremony. Gerry had to break the glass—a symbolic ritual performed by the husband—and Mr. Roach hadn't moved. Gerry tried several times to crack the glass which was wrapped in a linen napkin; once…twice…stomping on the glass forcefully with the heel of his shoe. It broke with a crash. Even this didn't jar the bug. Gerry had to act before the cockroach decided to scuttle across Steph's face. He flicked the stubborn roach with his finger and it landed on the edge of the veil behind Stephanie's back, poised to take a trip down the length of her gown. The flower girl standing next to Stephanie's rear shouted, "Bug…bug!" and there was pandemonium.

The guests stood up, hurriedly making their way to the aisles and out of the sanctuary, away from the wedding party that was left under the chuppah, dumbfounded.

Stephanie loudly yelled, "There's a bug! There's a bug!"

"A bug?" Gerry asked as if he didn't know anything.

Stephanie turned around and screamed, pulling off her veil and throwing it on the floor, kicking it away.

The young rabbi was beside himself, not knowing what to do, and so he laughed with some discomfort. The remaining guests joined him, laughing, and flashed their cameras, trying to capture the hysterical scene. The videographer was rolling and caught it all for Gerry and Stephanie's wedding video, to enjoy for years to come.

The reception that followed the roach incident was high-spirited and joyous. They danced, and perhaps drank a little more than they would have had it not been for the attendance of a member of the Roach family. By the end of the evening both Stephanie and Gerry were more than ready to go home to their apartment with armfuls of gifts and envelopes.

It was solely Gerry's apartment before they were married. He had lived there for five years while in school. The place was a true bachelor's pad until Stephanie arrived. Those were the days of weekend parties, dating, and watching Yankees games in rowdy sports bars.

After meeting Stephanie, however, the number of bachelor events decreased. He would take her to get-togethers with his friends at the apartment. They would have a couple of beers or a few glasses of wine while watching the game. Later, Gerry would walk Stephanie home. It was all quite romantic actually.

Gerry was fortunate in that he had a friend who gave him discount tickets. "It's who you know," he'd always say. Gerry thought, "Ah, Yankee Stadium…nights out with the guys—those were the days!"

But one of Gerry's fondest memories of that time was meeting Stephanie at a party. Their encounter was electric and became a story they often recalled, along with vignettes of their wedding day and honeymoon.

Their first night as a married couple was sedate compared to the excitement of their wedding. Both of them were exhausted from the frantic pace of the day. They couldn't wait for a late night treat of leftover buttercream wedding cake.

Stephanie was lounging on the puffy white comforter wearing her new lacy nightgown. It had been a gift from her Aunt Edith.

Meanwhile, Gerry was in the kitchen slicing a substantial piece of cake for them to share.

Stephanie shouted from the living room, "Be careful, don't drop any crumbs!"

"Wait!" Gerry said, dressed in his everyday plaid pajamas and wearing a smile that went from ear to ear. "Let's put on the video to remember honeymooning at home and our first piece of wedding cake in bed together."

"No, no!" Stephanie protested. "We've had enough videos taken to remember today."

But Gerry set up the camera anyway, saying "We want memories like this honey, to look back on when we are old and gray." He sat down on the side of the bed with his spoon in his hand.

Stephanie held onto the plate of cake and lifted her spoon to her mouth and was about to take a bite of the rich frosting when she looked down at the plate and gasped.

"C…C…Cockroach!" she screamed. She threw the piece of cake and the plate up in the air as she leaped out of the bedcovers and fled the bedroom yelling, "Not again!"

Gerry, not expecting this, was slow to move and found the piece of cake on his head, with buttercream running down the sides of his face, and a cockroach walking across his nose. Gerry jumped up, swatting at the cockroach to get it off his face. He looked quite funny, flailing his arms in the air in his attempts to get rid of the cockroach. He finally connected with it with his hand and sent the equally shocked cockroach flying across the room to a dresser top.

Gerry dashed out the same door that Stephanie had leaped through only minutes before. This was all caught on camera and would generate lots of laughter in years to come, but at the moment neither the bride nor the groom found it very humorous. Stephanie swore she would never have cake in the bedroom again nor would she get married ever again. Gerry liked that.

After many years of studying, Gerry has become a prominent corporate lawyer.

Stephanie is a graphic designer who took time off to be a stay-at-home mother to their spoiled 1-year-old daughter, Hannah.

They had added another addition to their family as well, Roger, a friendly brown and white beagle mix. He fit in so well because, like Gerry, he was quite passive and he never growled or snapped when Hannah would pull his ears or tail, or try to poke him in the eye. Roger would just get up and walk away to another room when Hannah's torture became too much to tolerate.

Gerry prefers city life with easy access to all amenities. He enjoys the excitement of the bright lights and the traffic sounds that lulled him to sleep every night.

Whereas Stephanie is drawn to the suburbs. She wants to mix with other stay-at-home moms and have play dates. She envisions herself organizing kids' parties and charity events, and introducing Gerry to the right people to further his career. She must reside in a suburb that is upper class but not snobbish.

She does not seem to realize that a combination of those two traits is never easy to stumble upon.

Stephanie admitted to herself that she would miss many things about Manhattan. She quite enjoyed dining out at the best restaurants and shopping within walking distance of her home. "Sale" was one of her favorite words.

She and Gerry had everything in their lives planned out perfectly, or so they thought. Gerry asked, "Stephanie, are you entirely sure you want to leave Manhattan? I would be satisfied with buying a condo before the house." Both Stephanie and her parents' answer came across loud and clear, "NO!"

"You forget we have a child," Stephanie chastised Gerry.

"Yes, I know you're right," Gerry responded. His voice echoed his disappointment. "Hannah needs a home with a yard, and so does Roger. Well, come to think of it, I could use a couple of putting greens with sand traps." Gerry was grinning from ear to ear. He was always the optimist and could make lemonade every time life handed him lemons.

"Oh, no you don't," Stephanie retorted. "Stay on the golf course. I don't want golf balls in my garden."

Stephanie was thrilled that this year Hannah would celebrate her first birthday in their spacious new home. It was a perfect opportunity for her to entertain in their new home with all their friends and relatives. Hannah's birthday, January 5th, would ring in the New Year on a joyful note. However, they decided to postpone celebrating Hanukkah until Christmastime, after the moving and unpacking was finished.

The menorah, a gift from Gerry's grandmother, would have to wait. Nana Guldstein was a bit offended by this because the family always celebrated the holiday punctually. Gerry managed to calm her nerves about the postponement by telling her what a wonderful Hanukkah celebration they would have in he and Stephanie's new home. Stephanie explained to her mother-in-law that the menorah was already packed away deep in a box somewhere amid all the good china, which only seemed to upset Nana Guldstein all over again.

"Well, then, come to our house and bring the gifts," Nana Guldstein suggested.

"No, Ma," Gerry said, "Even the gifts are packed. I'm sorry, but the holiday will have to wait."

"Hmmm," Nana Guldstein mumbled under her breath. It was her way of saying she disapproved but would accept the delay this one time. But although she would abide by the change, she still shook her head, muttering, "My poor Hannah, no Hanukkah."

"Oy vey, Ma. Please, no guilt trips," Gerry muttered, tired of being caught between his mother and his wife.

They had boxes piled to the ceiling for months in advance, and so many were filled with books.

Stephanie suggested that perhaps they had too many books. She argued, "Gerry, you should leave at least half of them behind. Give them to charity."

"Why would I spend all the money I did on those law books to reference them, only to leave half of them behind? Steph, what charity would want law books anyway?"

To put an end to the discussion, Gerry turned up the volume of the TV so that the sound would drown out her demands.

Stephanie chuckled under her breath. She knew Gerry's love of books made getting rid of them impossible.

Stephanie said to herself, "Little does he know that behind his back, I donate most of his paperbacks to charity. Some I will send off to England. My parents live in England and love to read. Since they are both retired, they have lots of time to partake in one of their favorite activities, reading books."

Stephanie's relatives had lived in England all their lives. But her parents immigrated to the States when she was a small child. They brought her up to be an American. Their decision to return to England to live closer to the rest of the family was a difficult one, and leaving their precious daughter was heart wrenching.

Gerry and Stephanie travelled to England once every year to visit her parents, who, of course, missed her terribly. Gerry stated, "I love to visit my wife's parents, but not for the reason you might think. It's not because I don't see them that often. I just love that all the pubs are nearby and they offer lots of varieties of beer and ales that I can't find at home."

Stephanie would spend her time there perusing the bric-a-brac shops, while Gerry haunted the small bookshops for old editions of books to add to his never-ending collection.

Their last visit had been filled with drama. Roger, their dog, and a stray cat got into a row at Stephanie's mother's cottage. Then her mother's adopted cat joined in the melee, darting helter-skelter through the kitchen.

All the humans could do was watch the dog and cats run around the kitchen: jumping on counters, smashing dishes, knocking over plants, and sending baskets of dried herbs and spices flying all over the floor to mix with the bottles of oil they had already knocked over and broken.

Stephanie's father shouted, "Stop this craziness right now, you silly animals!" But to no avail, the madness continued, with none of the animals paying an ounce of attention to what he had said.

The result was a salad on the floor that was very slippery and hazardous. Gerry tried to stop Roger, "Roger heel! Stop! Don't do that!" But Roger, taken up in the excitement of the chase of the cats, heard nothing. Gerry tried to grab Roger as he ran by on the counter top, but Roger's fur was covered in cooking oil, and Gerry found it to be like trying to catch a greased pig. He slipped, crashing into the ottoman where Steph's mom had set out a tray of steaming tea.

During this whole process, Roger bit the stray cat's tail. The cat leaped off the counter, meowing in pain, and slid from one end of the room to the other on the cooking oil slick on the floor, until it crashed into the wall on the other side of the room. The stray cat escaped by picking itself up off the floor after crashing into the wall, slowly tiptoeing across the oil-covered floor, and dashing out the open door—never to be heard from again. Stephanie's mom hid her face behind a dish towel.

Stephanie's father was enraged, "We have never had problems like this with our animals ever before. It is the addition of your Roger monster that caused this to happen today. He shan't be allowed in my house ever again…out, out he goes!"

As a result, Roger was banned from the house.

Roger didn't understand the situation but wasn't

perturbed at all. He lay down on the quilt Gerry had put out for him beside the garden. Gerry lay down on the quilt with Roger and patted Roger's head, feeling sorry for his buddy. "Poor Roger, you do what comes naturally to a dog, and then you are punished for it. We are both in the dog house, aren't we buddy? That hardly seems fair to me, when the cats are as much to blame for what happened as you are." Gerry sympathized with Roger. There had been many a time over the years that he felt certain that Stephanie's parents were going to exile him to their backyard as well, and today was definitely one of those times.

Roger slept and snored just like an old man for an hour and, upon waking, meandered into the garden, pulling apart some flowers and sampling Stephanie's father's tomato plants. Gerry got up off the quilt and quietly scolded Roger, not wanting to draw any attention to Roger's latest faux pas. "Roger, you mustn't eat my father-in-law's produce. He puts such pride in his producing of it, he is sure to get really angry and ban you from his property completely. So no eating the veggies anymore Rog," Gerry warned Roger in whispered tones.

When Stephanie's father noticed the devouring of his precious tomatoes, she said, "I am so sorry Father, the tomatoes looked so delicious that I couldn't help eating one. The only problem was that once I ate one, it was so sweet and succulent I just couldn't stop myself. Please Father, can you forgive me for my greediness." Had Stephanie's dad discovered it was Roger who ate the tomatoes, he would have insisted on caging him, and the only time Roger was ever caged was when they travelled. He was not the type of dog who particularly liked to be behind bars. "Good job," Gerry said, commending his wife for assuming the blame.

The broken dishes, oil, and spices that were scattered all over the floor had to wait. Their concern was for the family cat. Stephanie's parents took her to the vet, where she was stitched, bandaged, and forced to wear a cone around her neck.

This caused even more of a ruckus. The cat, now forced to use the indoor covered litter box, kept getting her cone caught on the sides of the box, finding herself trapped inside. She would "Meow" in panic and fear every time she got stuck in the litter box entrance. Several times, the humans in the house had to rescue her.

No matter how often Gerry told Roger to "STOP BARKING!" he would not stop.

Every time the cone hit against the back door, Roger would break out in an alarmed, "WOOF! WOOF!"

This would get the cat hissing, causing Roger to bark even more. Poor Roger was exiled outside for the remainder of their stay. Gerry assured Roger, "The next time we go away on a trip, you can stay with Grandpa Guldstein." Roger's tail wagged eagerly, as if he was being fed a slice of roast beef.

Stephanie tried to talk herself into the fact that it

was a good idea that she gave away her husband's books to her parents: "I feel good about giving away Gerry's books to my dad, because he has far more time to read and enjoy them than Gerry will have for many years to come. I know Gerry wouldn't approve if he knew, but I can't bring myself to move all those dusty old paperbacks to our new clean home. Besides, my dad will keep them safe for Gerry."

Stephanie had given her father the more fragile books when Gerry was out visiting the ale and beer shops, asking her parents to not mention to him that she had given the books to them. She told her dad there were a couple of boxes containing hardcovers that were on their way in the mail.

"Thank you, Stephanie, for bringing us this last treasure trove of books. They will keep us with our noses buried in books for quite some time," Stephanie's dad stated gratefully.

Both her parents stated, "But we do miss our girl so much, now that we only see you once a year. Hannah is growing so fast and it feels like we miss so much when we don't see her. But we shan't bother you and Gerry this year; with your move coming up, you certainly don't need us underfoot."

From the other side of the screen door that leads into the garden, Roger could be heard barking one time, which in his language meant, "Yes," and they chuckle loudly at Roger's canine comment.

The entire Guldstein family, including Roger in his kennel, returned to New York. After a very long international flight, they arrived home tired, suffering from jet lag, and all a little crabby as a result. Stephanie put aside the photographs of their crazy trip to add to the photo albums going to the new house.

Roger, who is so excited to be home, chases his own tail for a significant amount of time. He then asks, with a loud bark, to go out in their courtyard and check to see if anything has changed while he was gone.

While doing his tour, he makes sure to stop at every tree, bush, pole, and fence post, and mark it as his just in case anyone has forgotten. However, Roger doesn't realize that about halfway through his task he has run out of marker fluid and is now just lifting his leg on the last half of the items he had intended to mark. Roger doesn't realize that he is about to embark on a new adventure. He will have new territory, new grass and trees, when Gerry and Stephanie make their big move. Gerry tells Stephanie, "I hope Roger adjusts to his surroundings. He won't have the same butcher and pastry shops he can run to for his treats."

Stephanie, still feeling guilty and nervous about giving away Gerry's books, wonders if he'll recognize them at her parents' house during their trip next year. She consoles herself by thinking, "Nah, Gerry has so many books he'll probably never notice any are missing." She tells herself that over and over again, trying to convince herself that there will not be a confrontation with Gerry over his book collection.

Stephanie feels a slight pang of loss as she thinks about her favorite neighbors, Seth and Ben, the couple on the fourth floor.

Every New Year's Day they would knock on the Guldsteins' door and present them with a lemon meringue pie. Seth and Ben had made the pie especially for them. Gerry would announce, "This is absolutely the best recipe I've ever tasted in my life."

Seth and Ben were more than just neighbors, they were good friends. On numerous occasions Gerry and Stephanie went out to plays or dinner with them, all hilarious and laughter filled, because Ben was such a comic.

Steph would miss the parties they hosted on their roof deck, which were some of the best get-togethers she had ever attended—glitzy, masquerade style fests like Las Vegas after-parties.

"You must come and visit us, Seth and Ben. You are so much fun, and we'll miss you more than you can even imagine. As soon as we're settled, we'll be sending you an invitation to our new home," stated Gerry with a strong conviction.

When they had all said goodbye, Seth and Ben advised them, "We can't come until after we return from vacationing in Spain."

Ben promised, "When we do come, we'll bring Spanish wine as a housewarming gift—and be prepared, because when we visit we'll be staying for the weekend or longer."

"No problem," Gerry and Stephanie told them in sync, wearing huge smiles of anticipation. "And bring your funkiest pajamas for when we take photos."

The Guldsteins weren't planning on moving with anyone besides their small family and Roger, the "almost human" dog.

Lots of people offered to help them with their move. Nana wanted to help them pack and then ride with them in the car to the new house. Neighbors even offered to do so.

Gerry's response to his mother was to state clearly, and with no doubt, that he and Stephanie wanted to do this alone. "NO! NO! NO!" he said over and over again. "Ma, please! The neighbors understood on the first "no." There will be enough of us in the car. We've got it all planned and organized, and we'll see you there."

"Yeah, yeah, yeah," Nana protested, "I know you don't need me anymore!" Gerry had no patience for his mother's shtick, which was intended, as usual, to make him feel guilty.

Finally, it is moving day. The sun is just rising. The mountain of cartons is ready to haul. Gerry spots an open box on the counter about the size of a shoebox, and as he peers inside he sees crystal water glasses. "Phew, no bugs," he says. Awkwardly clasping the box with one hand, he lets it slip to the floor. The glasses shatter with a crunch.

"Honey!" Stephanie yells in her characteristic loud-but-sweet voice. "The moving truck is here! I have Hannah and Roger, so come on!"

Gerry pauses, thinking this is how it's going to be

from now on: one ear listening to his mother, the other to his wife. "Oy vey!" he exclaims. "Dad was right to call Mom a yenta all these years."

His phone is ringing and is relieved to get away from the ruckus to answer it. He hears Stephanie as he ends the call but doesn't reply. Carrying the box of broken glasses to the back porch, he hopes Stephanie won't discover it before they get on the road. "I'll figure out later what to say if she notices that they're missing," he thinks to himself, knowing it will be an exhausting day ahead.

He does a last walk-through of the apartment to be sure they haven't forgotten to pack anything. He stands with his hands on his hips; Gerry is proud of what he has accomplished and says silently to himself, "I have done an excellent job. With all the challenges, we are ready and on the way."

"I will miss this place!" he laments, apparently to the stark walls that echo his voice as they had done the first day he moved into the empty flat. "Good job, if I do say so myself! Looks brand-new!" His eyes dart sideways as he notices a tangle of dust moving across the hardwood floor. "Phew," he says, relieved. "For a sec I thought it was one of the resident roaches out for a daytime stroll."

Gerry loves the bathroom's vintage black-and-white tiled floor and heavy, old porcelain tub and toilet. He recalls the times he felt the cool tiles against his cheek when he'd had too much to drink.

Sweat stains his T-shirt, and his forehead is spotted with perspiration from working with the windows shut because Stephanie said Hannah would catch her death of cold if they were open. "It was okay for me to pass out. Even though the excessive heat from the oversized radiator created a brutal moving environment, I did it, and I'm proud I did," Gerry states out loud to himself.

Gerry knew Hannah wouldn't have gotten sick with the layers of clothing Steph had on her. His own mother used to dress him in layer upon layer until he could barely walk.

All of the boxes are marked and sealed extra tight. One last box is left on the lonely table. Gerry carefully places the box on the floor so he can push it to where the others are piled. The table will stay in the living room, where Gerry found it the day he moved in. *Now the new tenant can have it,* he thinks.

He goes into the kitchen for one last look. Memories overtake his thoughts. Memories of parties filled his mind, with scenes of friends wiping the counters and floors with paper towels because of the drinks they spilled. Then there was Roger watching for birds out the window, barking and leaping into the air as if he could catch them. Thoughts of his mother coming every day with supper the first week he moved in crowded his memories. That all stopped the evening she knocked expecting Gerry to answer and a girl came to the door scantily clad, shocking them both.

Gerry looks up at the tin ceiling Stephanie never cared for, and the classic schoolhouse light fixture he loved so much. He smiles as he walks out of the kitchen into the hallway, noticing how shiny the hardwood floors still are.

"I'm going to miss you," he laments with a sigh.

He gazes at the city view outside the floor-length windows. The movers' noise reverberates in the sun-filled, empty rooms.

"Hey guys, need some water?" he calls out to them.

"No thanks, we're good," they reply, and jokingly add "but how about a beer?"

Though sad as he reminisces about their wonderful times in the apartment, at the same time he feels elated about moving to Long Island, closer to his parents' home and his new, elite law firm.

For the briefest of moments, Gerry pictures his mother's smiling face and her happiness for him, but then he thinks of one more very important reason they are happy to leave… but now is not the time to bring it up.

The thought of it is repulsive, and—*kenahora*—he doesn't want to give a jinx to the apartment. He recalls the annoying clanging of the radiators when the heat was turned on and the poor water pressure in the shower that forever leaked, never quite turning off.

These were some of the things he wouldn't miss, like the upstairs tenants who he dubbed "the honeymooners." They would slam doors, screaming at one another for hours, and, without fail, Gerry and Stephanie would have to listen to their bouncing bedposts for the rest of the night. But worse yet, those visitors… Gerry would flip on the kitchen light and there they were, caught by surprise, waiting motionless for him to make the first move.

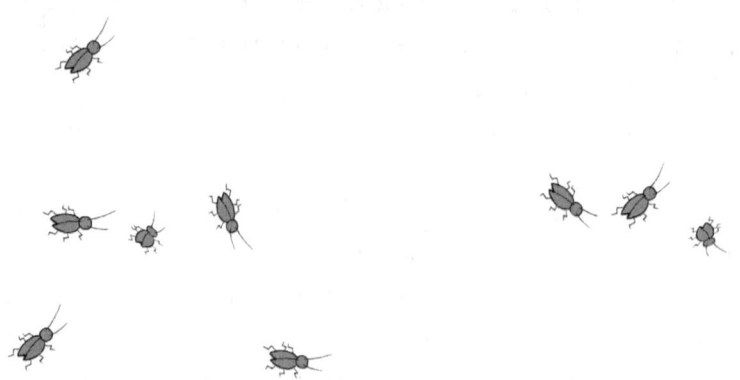

As Gerry walks down the steps of the old brownstone, he asks Stephanie, "We had some good times here, didn't we?"

"Of course we did," she agrees. "But the new house is amazing! I know we'll miss the convenience of the city and all of our close friends, but the new neighbors we met seem so friendly, and we won't have any more of those… well, you know, those 'uninvited guests' that came to our apartment over the past two years!"

"Yes," Gerry says, "you are certainly right about that! I can live without them, and it wasn't fun trying to get rid of those varmints."

"Now our old friends won't hesitate to visit us," Stephanie points out.

"Yes, true," he replied, "after Leslie jumped off the couch that night and tripped and banged her head, she never came back." "Okay by me," Gerry then muttered under his breath.

"What did you say, Gerr?" Stephanie asked. "Oh, nothing, Steph."

Roger is waiting by the stairs. He barks intermittently and hops up a stair and then down to let them know he is ready to go, and soon. He watches every movement Gerry makes, all the while wagging his tail so vigorously his entire body moves to and fro.

"Come here, Roger, let me put your sweater on you," Gerry says. He doesn't pay much attention to Roger's hesitation. Roger shakes his head from side to side, making it hard for Gerry to put his sweater on him. Roger hates the sweater Nana Guldstein made because it is too tight around his neck and it restricts him from scratching with his left paw, the left side being the side that is always itchy.

"Hey Roger!" Gerry tells him, "You look so handsome with your gear on!"

Roger is perplexed, and the furrow of his brow gives him a quizzical expression.

Gerry ignores Roger's predicament. "Atta boy," he says as he enthusiastically pats Roger's head. "I knew you'd like your sweater once it was on."

Roger walks away with his tail between his legs. Turning his head to catch a glimpse of Gerry, he passes gas to demonstrate how he really feels about wearing the sweater. This seals any doubt about his dislike for it.

Gerry holds his nose. "Oh, Rog, man!" he blurts. "What was that stink?"

Gerry and Stephanie are holding hands on the stairway. They gaze up at their apartment window one last time.

Roger sits, scratching his neck. He is signaling to have his sweater removed. Gerry jokingly asks Stephanie not to feed Roger any more liver treats.

"Okay, dear," she replies, "don't worry." She is thinking, *this is where Hannah was born—Manhattan.* She tells Gerry, "This was Hannah's first home, and she'll never remember it. What a sad thought. We do have lots of photographs though, and I'll tell her stories."

"Stories? About what, Steph?" he asks.

"Oh, stories about when we first met, our wedding…. Maybe we'll leave out some things," she said.

The glass chimes outside the window tinkle as a cold breeze passes by. "Steph, should we take those?"

"No," she replies, "They belong where they are on the tree."

"Stephanie, what were you saying about which stories?"

"Oh, never mind," she says, annoyed with her husband's endless questions. "We'll talk later…"

The glass of the chimes reflects the sun, bursting into a rainbow of colors. "Look, Gerry," Stephanie says, changing the subject. "It's so pretty, as if it were saying goodbye to us."

Everyone is ready to go. They pile inside the car, and all the seatbelts are fastened. Stephanie turns to Gerry.

"Do you remember Hannah's first bath?" she asks.

"I thought you said we'd talk later. This must be later. Really, Steph, how could I forget?" he responds, grinning. "I took the video, don't you remember? She splashed water all over the camera, and me! When we visit your mom and dad next year, we can play it for them, if they haven't already seen the email we sent them. Remember how she used to throw her oatmeal on the walls, and matted down Roger's fur with it?"

Gerry and Stephanie laugh about how Roger jumped in and the bath water spilled over, soaking the floor, leaking through to the apartment below, and covering Hannah's face with soapy suds. Then he darted through the apartment with a towel draped over him. They had been shocked at first, but then laughed at Roger's antics. They had boxes filled with

videos of Roger as a puppy, and now of Hannah—
more than enough to watch for years to come.

A ride in the car means a country drive to Roger.
He is bounding up and down from sheer excitement.
After Gerry puts a cover on the seat, Stephanie
hands Roger a bone from the kosher butcher's shop.
That does it—he calms right down. Roger
immediately begins to chew on it, savoring the
flavor.

Gerry and Stephanie never take their special car
out of the garage unless they are going on a long trip.
They live where the traffic zone is congested, and
Gerry is afraid the car will be touched or scratched
in that jam—even a bug, dust-speck, or fingerprint
drives him nuts. Walking from block to block is
sometimes faster and never becomes tiresome; so
much is there to see and hear. Roger plays in the
parks along the way, always running into the same
dogs he has met before and having fun, yap-fests, or
dogfights with them.

Gerry feared Hannah would be cranky while they
were stalled in traffic, but she is surprisingly docile,
playing with the toys Stephanie put in the back seat,
particularly the old jack-in-the-box her Granny gave
her. It once belonged to Stephanie's mom, and,
though it was a precious reminder of her own
childhood, she wanted Hannah to have it.

Roger barks and wags his tail as he chews on the
bone, pausing and scratching at his neck from time
to time. The gnawing usually irritates Stephanie, but
she is so excited today it doesn't bother her. Roger

was one year old when Gerry found him at a rescue center, the same time Stephanie started visiting him in his apartment.

After he met her, they dated for a while, and then she invited him to her apartment, where her cats, Stewie and Louie, greeted him at the door, purring and rubbing against his legs.

He told her he was allergic to cats. "I can't come in. I really have to go," he said, but she had a persuasive way about her and convinced him to stay for a while. By the time he left, his face and hands were swollen, and red blotches covered his arms. He was a sight to behold in those early days of their relationship. Benadryl saved the day, but he vowed never to return to Stephanie's apartment. They were so much in love, though, that she gave the cats to her roommate, who was more than happy to take them. Gerry, of course, never returned to that apartment.

"I never told you this before Steph, but I have wanted Stewie and Louie as my own ever since I moved in with you," Trudy, Stephanie's roommate, stated excitedly as her dream was finally coming true.

Trudy was obsessive about cats. Her last cat passed away before she moved in with Stephanie, and Trudy was heartbroken. In her bedroom, the curtains and bedspreads were decorated with cats. Cat pictures hung on the walls, and were splashed across book covers. Pictures of cats dotted her clothes and even her handbags had prints of cats. If anyone deserved to take Stephanie's cats, it was

Trudy.

Stephanie visited her cats every week, but certainly not with Gerry. She found them well cared for, even better than she had done.

"Trudy, I swear you spoil these cats worse than I did. You take fabulous care of them and I know I made the right decision when I entrusted you with their care." Stephanie constantly praised Trudy for tending to her cats with so much love.

She saw Stewie and Louis less and less after she began staying with Gerry at his apartment. When Roger came along, he stole her heart away.

Roger is an intelligent dog and easy to fall in love with. He always wears a bandana around his neck that says, "My Name is Roger. Beware, I Don't Like Cats."

Roger is like Predator when it comes to cats. He is well known throughout his Manhattan neighborhood. So well, in fact, that all of the cats run and hide when they see him coming.

The small shops, and even the postman, have treats for him. They call out, "Hey, Roger!" whenever they see him on the street. Roger knows who gives him treats and who doesn't; he would go get treats from his regulars even if they didn't call out to him. If the door of a store was closed, he'd bark until the owner would come with treat in hand.

The butcher knew about the move and packed

extra bones for Roger as a going-away present. He said, "Roger, I know you have a long trip ahead of you, and I want to make sure that you have enough bones to get you there, but also to keep me in your memory for a little longer than that." Roger, "BARK! BARK! BARKED!" as he left the butcher's after Stephanie said her goodbyes in Yiddish, a language Roger surprisingly understands.

Roger's pattern of barking makes it seem like he is actually speaking. When Gerry walks him in the park, he often talks to him the entire way, just the way he would speak to a person. Gerry always says, "Roger is a great listener! You can tell him anything and he will never break a secret."

Stephanie teases her husband and tells him that her facility for speaking "dog" is poor enough that he doesn't have to be concerned that Roger will spill his secrets. Gerry is as proud of Roger as he is of his daughter, his wife, and his personal accomplishments.

Gerry never lets Roger loose when cats are in Central Park, which happens only rarely, because the park has the reputation of being reserved for dogs.

One day, Roger had a scuffle with a cat there. Roger attached himself to the cat's leg and dragged the animal across the dirt until they were outside the gate. The cat's owner was infuriated and yelled at Roger, but he and his cat never returned to the park again. Roger barked fiercely as they departed from the park, like he was chief protector of his grassy domain.

Once, Stephanie took a video of Roger and Gerry walking and talking while she trailed behind with Hannah tucked in the stroller.

When Roger pulled at his leash, he got loose, chased a stray cat up a tree, and continued to bark ferociously as he stood at the foot of the tall oak tree. Gerry had to pull him away. The frightened cat climbed so high Gerry called the fire department to come and get it down.

"Ya, right," they told him. "Not in this city, buddy. Get a ladder." Stephanie and the rest of the family laughed at the movie, thinking it was hilarious, especially when Gerry split his pants trying to climb the tree to reach the cat.

When Roger was still young, Gerry and Stephanie took him to an obedience school, where he learned tricks and good manners. The instructor was so impressed with Roger's intelligence he suggested they take him to audition for commercials—but Gerry wanted a companion, not a star.

The obedience school course ended with a competition to determine which dog had learned the most. Roger took first place, which was enough to satisfy Gerry. He demonstrated how he could roll over, fetch the paper, and bring the cable remote to Gerry. He played dead. Roger also howls whenever Nana kvetches.

The instructor attached a blue ribbon to Roger's collar. As they were leaving, Roger ran ahead to show off to the people who knew him. When they went to the butcher's, Roger clenched the ribbon in his mouth for Mr. Shapiro, who gave him extra bones for his efforts. The ribbon now hangs in a frame on the wall.

Roger's repertoire includes: retrieving Hannah's toys and blanket; playing dead; and speaking on cue—one bark for "yes," two for "no."

He learned how to fetch *The New York Times* for Gerry. When he was thirsty, he nudged his water bowl across the kitchen floor with his snout until either Gerry or Stephanie would acknowledge him.

Two of Roger's more entertaining talents are fetching Gerry's Yankees T-shirt from his room and lapping up beer with Gerry and his dad when they watch sports on TV. When Roger got tipsy, he would crawl across Gerry's dad's legs and nap belly-up.

Roger is so smart he brings the empty beer carton to beg for more. As Gerry puts it, "Roger is cool and has a dog's buzz on."

"Gerr, you know Roger should not be given beer, it's not good for him and he gets woozy from it." "Well, so do I," Gerry tells Stephanie. Whenever she berates Gerry for giving Roger beer, Roger barks back at her until she realizes she can't win the battle.

When Roger finally wakes up from his stupor, he has become used to expecting a burger with sweet potato fries prepared by Stephanie, who knows the three of them anticipate the meal from the time the game begins.

Gerry's car receives attention wherever they go. It is a 1968 canary-yellow Buick Wildcat convertible that he had driven since high school and refurbished in his spare time during college. It is in mint condition, and strangers stop him on the street, wanting to ask all sorts of questions about it. "How did you restore it and still manage to find all the original materials that you needed to bring it back to its original condition?" questioned an admirer. "That's one of the good things about the internet," Gerry said, "it makes chasing down parts easier."

The father of one of Gerry's school friends has a shop in Brooklyn where the car repairs were made over the years. The car has a black leather interior and its jet-black cloth top is made of the best convertible material money can buy. Gerry's mother even had Hannah's car seat custom upholstered to match the bright yellow and black color theme of the car.

Needless to say, Gerry is proud of his car, and Stephanie appreciates it because of the pride of owning a vintage model. It has so much space inside, and, of course, the top goes down in spring and summer so she can tan on long trips to the country. Gerry particularly enjoys riding around in his convertible in the fresh air, but now, of course, its top is closed for warmth.

"Is everyone comfortable?" Gerry asks.

"Ruff!" Roger barks. Hannah repeats a few syllables for no reason in particular.

They say goodbye to the movers, who possibly

could be there before them if the Guldsteins make any stops or side-trips along the way. Not surprisingly, traffic backs up.

It is still early, before eight in the morning, and they have to stop by their storage unit to pick up a box Gerry left and make the final payment for renting the space. He is pleased about not having to pay for space anymore; the new house has a double garage with a room above. "That will be my storage area," Stephanie said. "No," Gerry replied, "it will be my office space. We'll see…"

While packing, he dreamed about storing his collectible cast cars and books in that extra space. He has about twenty cars, and his goal is to own every one ever made, particularly old Buicks. Stephanie has her own dreams to create an office space for herself.

They are planning to take a little time to stop for breakfast at one of their favorite restaurants just outside the city, an old-fashioned diner open twenty-four hours a day with the best homemade food. The waitress serves their food on old dishware. Dated photographs decorate the walls. Gerry is looking forward to their steaming pancakes, stacked on the plate with real butter and the highest quality Vermont maple syrup. Stephanie usually orders one of their famous omelets with cheese, spinach, and onions, and fresh homemade biscuits.

They decide to shop for the bulk of all the food they'll need to stock their new house later on during the week when the excitement of the move has abated. Gerry's foot is heavy on the pedal, and they probably will arrive at their new house ahead of schedule. He is relieved that Stephanie doesn't ask to stop at all the small stores along the way, as she usually does. The only ones open are convenience stores anyway.

The sky is crystal clear and blue. "I think it's supposed to snow tonight," Stephanie says. "I heard it on the news. What do you think, honey? Do you think it looks like snow?"

"I haven't heard the weather report yet, Steph, but it doesn't matter much, because we'll be in our new home with the heat on and the fireplace burning by the time it starts. Don't worry; we'll have enough to keep us busy while it snows."

Roger and Hannah are sleeping, and jazz music fills the car as they drive along in the winter sunshine. Gerry casually reaches over to the radio and switches to the station that plays only oldies he can sing along with. Stephanie immediately begins to blather—anything to divert his attention from the radio. His off-key voice irritates her, so as he begins to croon she fumbles with the dial and changes the station as if she had done it by mistake. He calmly asks her to put it back to the same station.

"I'll try, honey, but first can we listen to the news and weather?" she replies. He stops singing—he knows how much Stephanie dislikes his voice, particularly when he sings in the shower.

Every so often, in-between the radio and silence, Roger's distinctive snoring can be heard along with the off-key notes Gerry sings to annoy Stephanie for turning off the radio. The drive is otherwise peaceful.

Gerry feels a sudden wave of affection for his wife and grasps her hand in his own. She smiles contentedly, thinking the moment is perfect...now that he has stopped singing.

Both are excited by the prospect of their new home and a bright new year, both of which are almost upon them.

Chapter Two

LONG ISLAND BOUND

On the road, Gerry and Stephanie fondly reminisce about how free they used to be and how their circle of friends used to party with them on the weekends when the alcohol flowed, the chitchat buzzed, and they laughed and laughed.

"OMG," Stephanie says. "We already sound like our parents, talking about how life used to be."

Gerry grimaces. "We still enjoy ourselves," he replies, somewhat defensively.

"Yes we do, and always will," she affirms as she pinches his leg.

"I give in, I give in," he quips.

They are in high spirits. Since they moved in together, dressing for Halloween became a fun custom they planned long ahead of the holiday, a tradition they intend to keep. One year Ben was Fred Astaire and Seth was Ginger Rogers. Another Halloween, Seth was Marilyn Monroe and Ben was John F. Kennedy, and oh my, Seth was stunning!

Gerry asks Stephanie if she remembers one day in the summer when they visited their friend's beach house and played a game with water balloons.

"Of course," she replies. "The guys were blindfolded, and the girls stuffed water balloons into the tops of their bathing suits, and we all collided into one another, chest to chest, the girls slamming against the guys with all the strength they had to soak them when the balloons burst! I remember, because I had a sore chest the next few days."

"We did have fun, then," he says. They laugh out loud.

Stephanie says, "And remember how you scared me to death when you buried yourself in the sand, waited for evening, and grabbed my ankle pulling me down? I screamed and ran into the water while everyone laughed and took our picture. I thought you were a crab."

"Yes, we were more spontaneous then," she says, "no second thoughts about going places or doing things. Now we have to plan."

She pauses, and her face lights up. Sliding until she is sitting at the edge of her seat, she looks at Gerry's face and says, "Maybe we should keep on driving until we reach Florida. We'll call your mother to let the movers in and..."

"Stop!" snaps Gerry. "You know we can't do that

anymore. Let's get back to reality."

"Wow, Dad, have you changed! I'm only kidding. No, no, I take that back. I'm not kidding. I'd love to go."

"Me too," he confesses. "Me too!"

They both get serious and discuss which boxes they will open first once they arrive at their Long Island home. Stephanie suggests, "Why don't we open the boxes labeled 'bedroom' first. That way, if we become tired we will at least have blankets and pillows to sleep on."

"Wow honey! That is very smart thinking on your part." Gerry praises his wife for being so organized. He is in such good spirits he agrees with everything she says because he doesn't want to spoil their joyful mood.

As he listens to Stephanie, he realizes how much she sounds more and more like his mother. During the last few months they've been stressed, arguing about what to take with them. He stubbornly resisted her when she insisted upon throwing away his torn college khakis and T-shirts. He recalls his mother ditching his father's worn-out clothing, and his panic and anger whenever she did.

"Boy, we are starting to sound like my mom and dad," Gerry says. "I see it now."

Although Gerry and Stephanie don't agree on all subjects, early on in their relationship they agreed never to go to bed angry. It has always worked for them. "Kiss and make up," either would say to the other.

Gerry's mom and dad intend to visit right away and, as usual, will bring homemade food and pastries for everyone to enjoy on their move-in day. There was nothing that could keep them away. Stephanie looks forward to eating her mother-in-law's delicious strudel, appreciative of how difficult it is to make. Gerry's mother always insists upon bringing food, and there's no stopping her once she decides to do something.

Even when Grandpa Guldstein explodes, "Enough is enough! How much can a person eat?" Nana Guldstein would say, "Food never goes to waste, and it can always be put away for another day, or frozen for the future." "No, Ma, we don't freeze food so forget it," Gerry tells her.

Grandpa Guldstein knew when he was beat, and would simply nod his head and go back to what he had been doing before he lost his temper with Nana Guldstein. After all their years together, he had learned when to cut his losses.

Stephanie can't stop her mind from racing, and again reminds Gerry about emptying all the cardboard boxes and putting them outside as soon as possible, as the movers and the exterminators had recommended, so any critters that may have slipped into the boxes would not spread to their new house.

"Yes, my dear, I heard you...several times. I remember. Don't worry, I've got it!" Again, Gerry is irked at his wife's uncanny resemblance to his mother—both nagged him. He found himself suffering from "Jewish Mother Syndrome." Despite all his efforts to prevent it from happening, he seemed destined to live with "Jewish Mother Syndrome" for the rest of his life.

"Yes, I just want to remind you again, honey," Stephanie mutters as she chews a piece of candy.

Gerry brings the heel of his hand to his forehead. "Oy. I will do all of it when we are there, my dear."

Since living in New York, Stephanie panics at the sight of a small, crawly creature, be it a rat near the stairwell or an ant creeping across her desk. And God forbid when a spider should slither anywhere at all. When such events happen, she always leaves the apartment until Gerry has killed it and flushed it down the toilet.

One evening a few years back, when she returned home from work, she took a hot shower, as was her habit. Upon hearing Gerry enter the apartment she called out a loud "Hello" from the bathroom. "Be out in a few!" she shouted.

Once Gerry was settled in the living room, he poured himself a glass of wine to relax while waiting for Stephanie to join him.

Suddenly, he heard a piercing scream and jumped up with a jolt, knocking over the red wine onto the white wool Australian rug. Sprinting towards the bathroom with his heart racing, what he expected to find was an intruder fully armed and ready to hold them hostage while he sacked all their valuables.

Instead, there was Stephanie, bare to the bone, clutching the shower curtain around her like a shield. She let out a bloodcurdling shriek as she pointed to the floor, looking poised for a heart attack.

He took a deep breath. "A bug, Stephanie? It's a bug!"

"No, they're not bugs!" she screeched.

"Okay, they're not bugs. I'll get them, take it easy."

As he glanced back at her, he saw two more cockroaches on the curtain rod above her head. They were the largest roaches he'd ever seen. He hurriedly rolled up a *New York Times* that was in the rack beside the toilet and crushed the critters with it.

His heart rate eventually abated after drying up the red-stained rug, and he spent the remainder of the night consoling Stephanie with several glasses of wine. She twisted, turned, and then lay there, gazing at the shadows on the wall from the headlights of passing cars.

He never did tell her he'd spotted a couple of other bugs—one hanging from the chrome shower rod, the other lurking in the sink. He figured she would have moved out then and there had she known.

Neither forgot this incident, and Stephanie was so traumatized she took showers only when Gerry was in the room. The white rug, as it turned out, was permanently stained. He asked her to call out, "Bug!" rather than shriek the next time she saw a cockroach. Though she agreed to this in principle, she never could compose herself enough to say "bug" without screaming.

The trouble was, their old brownstone had eight units, which gave the cockroaches ample space to hide, mostly behind walls, appliances, TVs, even old books, and their favorite—inside boxes. Stephanie searched the apartment, trying to locate where the roaches came from. She went through each book page by page—no bugs.

She was surprised, however, when she discovered a photograph of one of Gerry's ex-girlfriends wearing a bikini. "Gerry, why do you still have a photograph of one of your ex-girlfriends wearing a bikini?" Stephanie questioned accusingly.

Gerry was caught off-guard by this, he swore to her that he had simply forgotten to throw it away. "This should have been thrown away a long time ago. After all, we have been married for years. That girl's breasts are so oversized for her frame. When did you last speak to her?" Stephanie questioned Gerry as if she was in interrogation mode. "I have not talked to that girl since we started dating. Also, she was very plastic and her breasts weren't even real, and I didn't like that fact one bit," said Gerry to pacify her. Reassured, Stephanie felt satisfied with her 34 C's, as was Gerry, though for a split second he admitted to himself that he had liked his ex's body. Back in college he and his friends always discussed their girlfriends' chests, and boy, did she have some hooters!

After that, he searched through the books himself before Stephanie packed the rest, finding nothing else incriminating, and certainly no bugs. She considered them so repugnant she was on a first-name basis with the neighborhood exterminators, Rick and John. The landlord told the exterminators to go to her apartment whenever she called because he couldn't deal with her hysteria.

The big moving day was almost upon them. Stephanie was finishing up her packing. She was in good spirits anticipating the imminent move, and she recalled pleasant memories as she wrapped their various belongings in newspaper and arranged them in the boxes. Then, out of nowhere, the memory of one particular night intruded upon her thoughts and sent shivers up and down her spine and made her hair stand on end.

She was in the pantry late one night after downing two strong cups of caffeinated coffee, and thought she spotted a roach running past her and over a loaf of raisin bread. She looked in the corners and crevices for the roach that inevitably appeared loitering on the shelves every night searching for a crumb to feast on. Although she was afraid of roaches, she had built up enough courage to try running each one down and squashing it with a paper towel. Anticipating which escape route it might suddenly take, she would aim the paper towel slightly ahead of the roach and try to pulverize it. She was obsessed with killing the critter and wouldn't sleep quite as well if she missed.

There he was…running speedily undercover behind a box of Irish oatmeal. Tripping on her slipper then falling over a stool, she sprang to her feet waiting for the roach to show itself. Rather than admit defeat, Stephanie decided to coax the roach out of hiding by spraying a can of insect killer between the shelves.

A minute or two passed...and then...out came...not one, not two, but at least thirty oversized cockroaches crawling and scuttling over one another, travelling across the shelves, down the lower levels to the floor! Stephanie jumped back and was sickened by the sight of the slimy brown creatures. She found herself standing next to a sea of cockroaches, screaming insanely for Gerry.

Completely shocked by the number of roaches that lived behind the walls of the pantry, she went flying into the bedroom to wake Gerry and, breathlessly, she told him what had happened. "Oh what have I done?" she moaned.

Gerry went into the kitchen reluctantly, not knowing what he would find or what to do. He grabbed the roach killer and sprayed the pantry floor until there was nothing left in the cans. After a while they no longer crawled or moved, and it was clear the roach killer had done its job. Gerry swept up the mess with a broom and disposed of the cockroaches in a plastic bag he sent sailing down the garbage chute.

Stephanie huddled in a wing chair, hugging her knees, afraid to set foot on the floor or go to sleep. Gerry stayed up sitting close to her until morning. "Yes, Steph...okay Steph...whatever you want Steph," were his answers to any and all of the qualms his wife expressed throughout the rest of that long night. "Yes, Steph, we'll move," he promised her. She still cringes whenever she recalls the cockroaches parading down the shelves and walls forming a pool of wriggling insects on the pantry room floor.

Before their moving day, Gerry and Stephanie knocked on the doors of their new Long Island neighbors, informing them they were moving in early on Christmas Eve day, wanting to be respectful of them by not making noise on the holidays. Many were not home. The family that lived on one side of their house had left the cold weather and was in their winter home in Santa Barbara for the holidays. The family on the other side had invited all of their relatives and friends to celebrate the holidays on Christmas Day, as was their yearly custom.

The Wilkersens invited Gerry and Stephanie to their annual Christmas party. They were extremely wealthy and gave the air of snobs, but seemed friendly enough when they first met. They also told the Guldsteins they usually went to Las Vegas for New Year's Eve.

The Guldsteins were impressed with their new next-door neighbors' plans. The Wilkersens had an indoor heated swimming pool, with a retractable roof overhead, and French doors that opened onto the lawn in the summer. They gave the Guldsteins permission to use their pool any time they wanted to until they built a pool of their own. Gerry and Stephanie had already discussed the prospect of putting in a pool when Hannah turned five, so they thanked the Wilkersens for their generous offer.

Gerry couldn't help mentioning that he and Stephanie always went to his mother's house in the summer, where she had an Olympic-sized pool in the back yard. He interpreted the Wilkersens' remark about building their own pool as an imperative for all members of the neighborhood.

Nudge, nudge—Stephanie elbowed Gerry, saying, "Did you have to add the size of your mother's pool?"

"Yes, I did," he said. "They practically told us to put in a pool." "No, not necessarily, Gerr."

Gerry and Stephanie speak about making time to go to the Wilkersens' party despite all the cartons they have to empty and all the furniture arrangement they have to do.

Hannah and Roger are still sleeping in the back seat. Roger is dreaming, whimpering as he breathes in and out, occasionally barking. Hannah is quiet. Stephanie tickles Hannah's feet, and Hannah giggles as she sleeps.

They are almost there. Gerry feels anxious. Stephanie is talking a mile a minute. He tuned out her voice several miles back in the same way he blocks out his mother when she harasses him. He interrupts her once in a while, saying, "Yes dear, you're right," but she knows his response is automatic and in fact he is not listening to her at all. To prove her point, she stops talking, but he continues to say, "Yes, dear, you're right!" She is ever so familiar with his ploys and laughs.

"I hope you realize that you just said 'yes dear,

you're right,' when I didn't even say anything at all. If you are not going to listen, then at least pay attention to know exactly when I quit talking."

"Yes, ma'am," Gerry said, as he gave his wife a military salute.

Chapter Three

FINALLY THERE

Gerry and Stephanie stop at two small supermarkets to buy fresh fruit, snacks, and juice, as well as breakfast food to tide them over for the next few days. Stephanie is being fussy, as she usually is about supermarkets—the store has to be just the right type of place. In Manhattan, she would shop at different markets that specialized in certain foods: the freshest fruits and vegetables from one market, meats from only the kosher butchers, breads and Italian pastries from small bakery shops, vegan cupcakes from gourmet specialty shops. Gerry cautions her not to buy too much, because his mom probably filled the fridge already. Stephanie knows he is right, but she still wants her specialty items his mom won't be bringing, and besides, she likes to explore new shops. Assuming she wants to window-shop, Gerry tells her there will be weekends after New Year's Day for them to visit the small towns and shops. She knows that, but tells him, "I understand all the stores are closed. Why can't we just take a look anyway?"

"No, Steph," Gerry says, "we have to be at the house, so the movers won't have to wait."

Hannah stretches as she wakes, gurgling and forming syllables, speaking her own language combined with the few words she knows. She is now wide-awake and hungry—her face turns a bright red, and she screeches, "Cookie! Cookie!"

"Okay, okay," Stephanie tells her as she pulls a vegan carrot cookie from the bag she is holding. Hannah immediately collects herself and says, "Tank you, Mama."

Roger is hungry, as always, and barks to make his needs known. He emits two low barks, then a string of loud, eager yaps, followed by a long howl. "Okay, boy, I realize you have to go…." Gerry takes him out for a short walk while Stephanie goes shopping with Hannah.

After shopping, one bag of groceries has turned into several. While Stephanie arranges them on the car floor, Gerry's mother calls on the phone. "Now, don't buy anything," she says. "I'll bring everything!"

Gerry points at his wife. "See, I told you!" he remarks. "Look at all of this food. We'll need another refrigerator."

"Not to worry," she whispers. "Most of the food

isn't perishable—just some unusual teas and rye crackers." She devours a cracker she has taken out of the box. "You'll love them," she says, waving one under Gerry's nose. He makes a gesture for her to stop. Still on the phone, he replies with a gradual crescendo of his voice, "I knew you would stock the kitchen and cook for us. I can always depend on you, Ma! I'd wager the kitchen cabinets are full!"

"Yes," she answers, "of course, did you think otherwise? What kind of mother would I be if I didn't do that?"

"Why would I think otherwise?" he asks, grinning broadly at his mother's question.

Even in Manhattan, Nana would prepare full-course meals she would bring with her. Whenever she visited, she would bring along grocery bags full of food, all kosher. Stephanie made exceptions when it came to buying kosher fare, especially when she went to the French bakery for her warm croissants and to the Italian bakery for her irresistible cannoli. Gerry expected his mother to bring his favorite apple raisin strudel each time she came to his house and was never disappointed.

The elder Guldsteins would only go to exclusive kosher Chinese restaurants in Manhattan and, of course, to kosher delicatessens.

Gerry jokes that the noise level in the restaurants is comparable only to the noise level on an El Al plane flight to Israel—a cacophony of talking and praying that gives Gerry and his dad indigestion. They depend on large bottles of Tums to save the day.

"Is that your mother on the phone?" Stephanie demands loudly, though she knows the answer.

"Yes it is," Gerry states matter-of-factly, wearing a smug expression. "Who else would it be at this hour?"

"And I suppose she has more than enough food for us?" Stephanie inquires, though quite certain of the answer.

"Yes, of course, dear," he perfunctorily replies as he holds the phone slightly away from his ear because his mother's voice is so shrill and her conversation so monotonous. Try as he might, he cannot find a pause in the conversation where he can safely say goodbye.

"They're already at the house?" Stephanie surmises.

Gerry nods at her and tells his mom, "Stephanie needs help with the baby. I have to go! Love you, bye!" He shuts off his phone abruptly.

Stephanie and Gerry laugh and joke about Nana's nonstop chatter. In the back of his mind, Gerry pictures the expression on his father's face when he has had enough of his wife's babble. He recalls his grandfather's words at his bar mitzvah about marrying a nice Jewish girl: "Your dad married one, and so did I, and now look—such wonderful years of bliss."

Hannah and Roger are huddled side by side, listening intently to the conversation. Hannah leans over her car seat repeatedly, tapping the top of

Roger's head, making him wince. She tugs at his fur, and he shakes to break loose from her grip. His hind legs are flush against the back seat. He pokes out his snout next to Stephanie's ear and nudges her as he edges closer to the front seat to escape Hannah's torture. His brow is wrinkled, and his eyes look imploringly at Stephanie, as if begging her to rescue him. She turns toward him, and he barks, "Ruff! Ruff!"

"Is Hannah bothering you?" she asks. "Poor pup. I'll make it better. Here, Hannah, Mommy has another cookie to keep you busy, and one for you too, Roger."

Roger wags his tail forcefully, snatches the cookie in his mouth, and sits down. Hannah shrieks into his ear, upset he is out of reach. Roger growls and moves as far from the car seat as he can possibly get. He is finally peaceful, now that Hannah has stopped pestering him.

Stephanie gives Hannah a smile and rubs her leg as she kicks it back and forth. Roger wags his tail in victory, as if to say, "You can't get me now!"

Gerry sings off-key to his wide-eyed little girl as Stephanie takes his hand, and for an instant their eyes meet and they smile at each other. But she cannot endure her husband's lousy voice a moment longer, and leans forward to turn the knob to off.

"Hey, hey, what's that about?" Gerry asks.

"Look, we're almost there," she tells him. "I think that silence would be nice." Paying little attention to her request, he belts out a few more discordant notes. Stephanie cups her hands over her ears while Roger howls along with Gerry. Then, out of respect for his wife, he stops. Roger ceases his howling.

They gaze out the windows. Stephanie notices fewer houses decorated for the holidays compared to the city's festive lights on buildings, trees, everywhere. They turn to each other at the same moment and, with the same thought, exclaim, "I miss our apartment!" They break out in laughter.

"There's our house!" Gerry suddenly proclaims, pointing his finger at it. Sensing the excitement, Roger barks, bounds over Hannah's kicking legs, and fixes his gaze out the window of her door, happily wagging his tail. He jumps from one side of the car to the other.

"Roger!" Gerry orders. "Down!"

For a moment Gerry and Stephanie are distracted by the Wilkersens' lawn, where a vintage red sleigh stands, strung with white bulbs. A huge wreath of fresh red poinsettias adorns their front door. The house is elaborately decorated, looking merrily festive even in daylight.

"When it's dark and our neighbors flip on their lights the ambience will be incomparable," Stephanie tells Gerry.

"The lights on the buildings in the city could never recreate this scene," he replies softly, excited that Hannah will be able to see the lights from both her room and the living-room couch because all of their front windows face the Wilkersens' house.

The view from the rear is outstanding as well—conservation land with a narrow waterway. "No more brick walls or traffic with the constant beeping of cars and taxis, neighbors' shouting, music blasting and cigarette smoke drifting through our windows," Stephanie says proudly. "And no more little friends."

As they pull right up to their front door, Gerry's mother runs toward the car, her face glowing with the pride of a new grandmother. Stephanie feels a twinge of sadness as she thinks about her parents far away in England, and her cousins on the West Coast.

"Hon, I miss my mom and dad," she confides in Gerry. Roger touches her arm with his paw.

"Let's Skype them tomorrow," Gerry suggests.

This New Year's celebration will be low-key, she thinks, *with their friends away and only Gerry's family there.* His father, wearing a thick cardigan without a coat, is already out on the driveway as the car rolls to a stop. He gazes through the back window at his precious granddaughter, making funny faces to her expressions of delight as she kicks her legs and waves her arms.

"Gampa! Gampa!" she cries out.

Stephanie opens the door, and Roger leaps out of the car onto the snowy gravel of the circular driveway. He falters slightly after tripping over himself but is back on all fours in an instant. He shakes and propels himself into the air, twirling around, though no one is watching him—they are far more interested in Hannah.

"There's our baby!" coo Nana and Grandpa to

their granddaughter.

Gerry doesn't appreciate their baby talk. After all, Hannah is a year old and is already her own little person.

Frustrated with jealousy of Hannah, Roger barks and runs in circles, chasing his tail. Failing to get anyone's attention, he lies down on his back with his legs in the air, playing dead.

"Oh my God!" Stephanie cries out to Gerry, "Roger is sick!"

Gerry and his father roar with laughter. "Honey, Roger's not sick! He's playing dead."

Roger opens his eyes. Grandpa massages Roger's stomach and all is well except for Stephanie, who has fallen for Roger's trick again. "Get inside!" she snaps. "You scared me to death!"

Roger gets to his feet and tucks his tail between his legs.

"Oh, Roger, you do this to me every time. Bad boy!"

"Okay, okay, let's go in," says Grandpa, who takes Hannah in his arms and hugs her. Nana embraces both of them. "How's my princess?" he asks.

"Nana," Hannah manages to respond. "Gampa."

As Gerry walks to the door, he pats Roger's head to calm him down. "It's okay, Rog. I saw you jump in the air. We'll play later."

Gazing at Stephanie, Roger emits a low, muffled growl from the back of his throat.

"Don't worry, honey," Gerry says to his wife.

"He'll come around. He's insulted you don't like his tricks."

"Ruff!" Roger barks.

The weather is cold, and Gerry hurries everyone so he can take a photograph of them at the front door of the new house. Roger sits obediently in the middle and everyone smiles for the camera.

"Wait!" Gerry calls out. He sprints to his car, snatches the Yankees cap from the ledge of the back window, runs back, and balances the cap on top of Roger's head. Grateful for the attention he's finally getting, Roger happily licks Gerry's hand.

"Click!" shouts Gerry as he snaps the family portrait.

Stephanie turns to open the door as they hear the rumble of a large truck from down the road. "The truck is here!" Gerry exclaims. "Right on time!"

Their long anticipation and preparation to move into their new home is finally over.

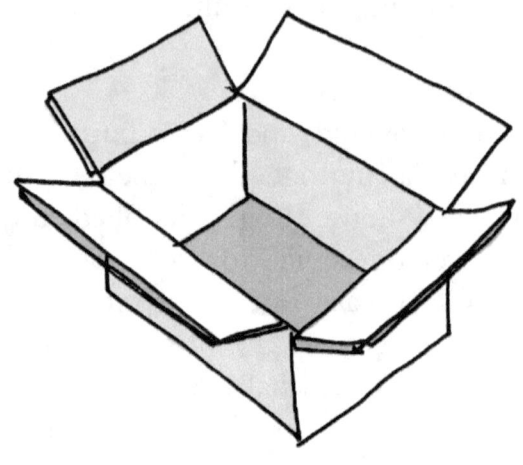

Chapter Four

TIME TO UNPACK

Nana hastily enters the house and heads for her favorite room, the kitchen. She pauses at the door to change into her slippers—the ones Roger steals and hides whenever she leaves them on the floor. She slices the bagels to serve with the lox and cream cheese and begins frying the potato latkes.

Her signature dish of a half grapefruit topped with a maraschino cherry is on the table. Gerry, who cannot stand sliced grapefruit with or without a cherry, makes his traditional comment, "Who was the person who began serving this dish?" Nana doesn't mind that Gerry never eats her grapefruit—she serves it anyway. When she thinks no one else is watching, she slides the grapefruit to Grandpa to

CHRISTMAS WITH THE COCKROACHES

finish, though he never does, and Roger cannot spit out the bitter stuff fast enough.

"It was not your mother, but someone just like your mother—a clone of her, perhaps," quips Gerry's father. Stephanie giggles. Nana shushes him to be quiet. Everyone laughs, including Hannah, who giggles just like her mother.

Nana makes fresh coffee for everyone except Stephanie, whose favorite drink is Jasmine tea with honey and a slice of orange. She brought all of the ingredients along and hid her own tea in the far corner cabinet and stashed the oranges in a paper bag at the rear of the fruit bin in the refrigerator. She makes certain not to tell her mother-in-law she stopped to buy her own tea and oranges, knowing Nana would be heartbroken if she knew. The oranges Nana brought were shipped from her friend in Florida, so of course they are considered special.

The movers are loitering around the kitchen, waiting for instructions, grateful for their paper cups of coffee. Nana set aside thirty dollars for each of them as holiday tips.

Hannah has French toast dipped in cinnamon— her favorite. "Mmmm," she murmurs as she picks up the perfectly cut pieces to indulge in them. With her empty hand she grabs her vintage plastic Goofy cup filled with milk. Each time she uses this cup, Nana coos, "This was your daddy's cup when he was a baby." Hannah is still too young to understand, but Nana says it without fail. All Hannah wants is the cold milk anyway.

Grandpa is chef to Roger, mixing ground turkey and scrambled eggs together with his dry food—his top favorite. Roger's next favorite is spaghetti and meatballs. The sauce covers his snout all the way to his eyes, leaving little doubt about what he has been eating. Grandpa had filled a Tupperware container with spaghetti for Roger and Hannah to share later in the week.

While waiting for his meal, Roger sits, lifting his paws into a begging position. He is like a hog that loves to eat everything indiscriminately. "Roger the Moocher," Grandpa and Gerry often call him.

When it's Thanksgiving, he somehow knows it, and patiently awaits his feast of turkey, mashed potatoes, stuffing, and Nana's specialty of green and yellow string beans with baby onions. Roger is particularly fond of baby onions, rolling them inside his mouth before chewing down on them. Unfortunately, they give his breath a distinctly pungent odor—and, of course, this is when he wants to "give kisses," at which time Stephanie tells him, "Yuck, stay away from me!" Gerry pushes his face away too, hurting Roger's feelings.

Then Roger goes to Hannah, because she can be relied upon not to show prejudice. He lovingly licks her face, leaving the stench of onions on her cheeks while she laughs and giggles in delight. Grandpa is smart and always carries dog biscuits made especially for dogs' breath whenever he cooks for Roger. After Roger eats his breath biscuit, Grandpa is the next person to get Roger's "kisses." Grandpa rubs his belly and tells him what a good boy he is.

Roger is just as spoiled as he was before Hannah was born. His plush bed has a pillow Nana embroidered with his name. He also boasts a cookie jar lettered with the saying "Paws Off," that Nana made in pottery class.

Stephanie's mom and dad send a box of homemade English dog biscuits every Hanukkah, and when the package arrives, Steph places it in the middle of the living room floor for Roger to sniff. Somehow he knows when to expect his biscuits and rushes to the front door when the mailman is coming. Roger will have to get accustomed to a new mailman, now that he is the guardian of new territory—hopefully with minimal barking or fuss.

"Ma, what do you think of the house?" Stephanie asks her mother-in-law.

"Well, dear, Grandpa and I inspected every foot while we were waiting for you, and both of us think it's more beautiful than when we saw it the first time."

"Yes, it's more beautiful to me too," Stephanie remarks. "I love it! I'm so glad the kitchen isn't like most kitchens in new homes, with cabinets that are boring brown wood and beige granite on the counters. The black and white and red glass tiles are unique."

"I love the colors in the kitchen too, dear," Nana adds. "They're so different and alive. And the bathrooms! Rooms a person could easily stay in for hours! Don't keep any magazines in there, or

Grandpa and Gerry will never move off of their thrones!" They all laugh loudly.

Both are so engrossed in their conversation that Stephanie nearly forgets about the movers, who are still waiting for her outside by the open door to receive their instructions. They must finish before 3 p.m. because they have one more stop before going home for Christmas Eve.

"Oh, damn it," she thinks, "they are on the clock." She tells her mother-in-law, "I have to go. We'll talk later, Ma."

She goes to the door, where some of the guys are outside, unloading boxes from the truck. The moving company owner tells her his guys don't know where to put the furniture. "Could you tell us, please?" he asks.

"Yes, coming!" She turns back to Nana. "Ma, I'll be back. Will you watch Hannah while I give directions? Don't worry, I won't forget. I'll get their coffee."

Stephanie is itching for the movers to take her furniture inside. She can't wait to set up her new home, and she worries the movers won't be able to finish by their deadline, so she goes outside to join them. A freezing draft flows in through the front double doors. Gerry commands Roger to stay in the kitchen. The dog lies down immediately, albeit with a mournful howl and one paw across his snout.

Gerry and his father join in to help supervise the movers, who now are in every room of the enormous house. Stephanie continually points at the places she wants the furniture to go. "Over here. Maybe over there. I'll decide in a few minutes." She wears an apprehensive expression, not wanting to place the furniture where it doesn't belong and then having to move it later. Boxes are everywhere. She can't keep track of what's in them because the movers are working so fast. Panicking, she widens her eyes and glances around at each box as if expecting something to jump out at her at any moment.

Nana pesters the movers with questions about whether they're married, what they plan to do for the holiday, even what their plans are for New Year's. She doesn't stop talking, though several of them speak no English. In their own language they fret about how this woman won't shut up. Gerry catches a Spanish phrase here and there. Some are laughing, and a few are polite, smiling and trying to answer her as best they can, despite working under time constraints.

Nana offers them pastries. Gerry finally puts his foot down. "Ma, enough already!" he yells. "These guys have to get back, and we want to move in *today*, not next Christmas! Maybe you could take Hannah to her room to play."

"Sure, I can tell you want to get rid of me!" she retorts with her usual shtick.

Stephanie has the movers take Hannah's boxes of toys to her room. Nana reassures Stephanie not to worry about Hannah. She will take her upstairs when she shows the moving men where the boxes go.

"Come to Grandma, my precious, away from your mean daddy!" Nana mumbles under her breath. "Let's go upstairs!" she calls to Grandpa.

"Coming, dear," he replies.

"Dad! Dad!" Gerry calls. "Here is a pair of scissors to open the boxes, but please remember to put the empty ones in the hallway!"

"Yes son, I hear you. I'm not your mother!"

"Don't forget, Mom, you too, please!"

Nana takes Hannah aside and whispers to her, "Your mommy and daddy are *meshugena*—crazy!"

"Ma, the boxes go in the hallway, or Stephanie will become nervous!" Gerry demands.

"She will become nervous?" Nana responds. "Why would boxes make her nervous? Is there something I should know? Did she have a bad childhood experience? Are there dead bodies in them?"

"Ha-ha, very funny, Ma," he replies sarcastically.

Hannah climbs upstairs reluctantly, balancing on each foot as she goes, as Nana coaxes her up. "Here, I have your favorite cookie, and then we will take your toys out of the boxes!"

When Hannah hears the word "toys," she grasps onto Nana's hand to help herself go up the long, curved stairway faster. Up they go, step by step.

"Toys, Nana, toys!"

The movers finally prepare to go back to the city for their last job. Nana hands them their tips, as well as packages of her homemade cookies for their families. The house is cold from the doors staying open for so long, even though Stephanie turned up the heat.

Gerry stares at Stephanie. Each knows what the other is thinking. *The boxes…the boxes! We must get the boxes out of the house!*

Gerry's parents are upstairs with Hannah, unpacking her clothes and putting the empty cartons in the hallway as they were told to do. Gerry's mom is still grumbling to herself about the cartons. She cannot keep quiet.

"Maybe our daughter-in-law takes medication for this sickness? Maybe there is a name for it? I have to find out from Gerry later on in private."

"Mind your own business, please!" Grandpa says, exasperated.

"I certainly don't want Stephanie to panic. I just don't understand the reason everything has to be unpacked in one night," mumbled Nana loudly in confusion.

Grandpa, baffled, doesn't fully understand either. Stephanie wants all the boxes crushed and put outside far back in the yard until they are disposed of on the day after Christmas. She and Gerry do just that, carrying the boxes and leaning them against the neighbor's fence, far away from their own home.

"Such *meshugenas!*" Nana mutters, knocking her forehead with the heel of her hand.

Grandpa approaches Gerry and asks, "Why not put the cardboard in the garage like most sane people? When your neighbors see that mess, I'm sure they won't be happy about it, especially on their

Christmas holiday."

"That's true Dad, but I don't want to clutter the garage," Gerry lies.

"Clutter an empty garage? What could you clutter? You could fit the entire neighborhood's trash in there for months."

Grandpa nonetheless obliges, raising his shoulders and eyebrows. Nana overhears the conversation. She feels she just has to say something.

"Are you both crazy? Look at that mess! A person would think you have bugs!" she declares. Grandpa laughs loudly at the outrageousness of her statement.

"Don't be silly," says Gerry, with a tremor in his voice. "We don't have bugs. Stephanie hates boxes, and that's all!" he insists.

"So what do I know, anyway?" Grandpa asks.

"I still think they both need help, but what do I know?" said Nana. "I know just as much as your father."

Chapter Five

CHRISTMAS EVE

Nana has finished Hannah's entire room, putting away all her clothes and toys and, with Grandpa's help, hanging her shades and pictures. Hannah topples things over as she runs around her room, carrying her jack-in-the-box in one hand and dragging her baby blanket with the other. She places the jack-in-the-box down on the rug directly in front of Nana, and without warning it pops up, startling Nana, who holds her hand over her heart, breathing with effort.

Hannah giggles and drops her blanket, pointing at the pieces of the rocking horse Grandpa is attempting to assemble. She whines, letting him know this is one of her favorite toys and she might have a tantrum if he can't put it all together.

"Don't worry your pretty little head," Grandpa tells her. "Your horse will be done in a jiff! Play with your grandma."

After two hours of strained concentration, the horse is almost finished. Hannah pouts and cries crocodile tears while Grandpa keeps working, but it's not too long before she is onboard, happily rocking back and forth.

When all is done, they head downstairs. Hannah pulls Nana's hand, leading her into the dining room, then into the living room, which has windows so tall they nearly reach from floor to ceiling. Hannah stares out one of the windows, watching the lights flicker on the Wilkersens' lawn with rapt attention.

Nana picks up the camera and captures the moment. "I am so proud of our son, and it's a blessing he lives so close by," she says.

Grandpa nods, acknowledging their good luck, and kisses his wife on the cheek.

Gerry and Stephanie file in and out of the front doors, hauling empty boxes outside. They watch as the caterers bring food inside the Wilkersens' house for the next day's holiday party. Gerry suddenly has to stop his parents from rushing outside in the cold to introduce themselves to the new neighbors. Barring his mother with his arm, he says, "Not now, Ma, later, please?"

"We were just going to say a quick hello," his dad says.

"Yeah, a quick hello that would turn into an

hour," says Gerry. "Go over after the holidays, when they aren't so busy."

He is impressed with the extravagant amount of food carried into the Wilkersens'. He thinks they must have at least two refrigerators, maybe three. "Do you think we should stop by tomorrow late in the evening?" he asks Stephanie.

"Yes, of course we should," she says. "They're our new neighbors. It's great having friends next door."

Gerry's mom calls them inside to eat an early dinner. "All your boxes are out! You can relax now, can't you? I don't mean to interfere, but what if Grandpa and I take the boxes to our house to put out with the trash so they're not in your yard?"

"No!" Gerry and Stephanie snap in unison. "No, leave them alone!"

Nana is surprised at their intensity. "You don't have to scream, you know," she says. "I'm right here. Do you have the same illness as your wife maybe?"

"Ma, please!" Gerry pleads. "We are not sick."

"Okay, so I won't instigate anymore. *Mazel tov,* enjoy your new house!" she replies with her trademark sarcasm.

"What does your mother mean?" Stephanie whispers to her husband. "Does she think I'm crazy?"

"No, calm down, Steph."

"I am just trying to help!" Nana says in exasperation as she throws her arms up in the air.

Stephanie feels badly for being short with her mother-in-law, but now is not the time to discuss the boxes.

While the Guldsteins are eating dinner, the caterers next door finish their deliveries and the Wilkersens leave for their Christmas Eve ritual dinner and play in the city. All of them are dressed up; even their two teenaged children are wearing formal, fashionable clothing that makes them look like models in a magazine. The sky is clear, and the stars glitter, even though snow is predicted to arrive later in the evening or early in the morning.

Murphy, the Wilkersens' handsome yellow lab, is resting by the fireplace, opening one eye from time to time to check his surroundings. Every Christmas Eve they bring him leftovers from the restaurant. It was usually a prime rib bone.

Like Roger, Murphy is a pampered dog, and, though well behaved, he barked incessantly while Gerry and Stephanie brought out their empty boxes and leaned them in a corner against the Wilkersens' wrought-iron fence. The Wilkersens paid no attention to Murphy's barking, assuming their high-strung pet was merely making noise about the new neighbors moving in. Once the Guldsteins finished putting out their boxes, Murphy ceased his barking and peacefully wandered away from the window to his usual winter spot at the foot of the sofa in front of the fireplace.

Roger wasn't the least bit bothered by the sound of another dog barking. It was rare that Roger reacted to any noise, for that matter. After all, Roger was a city-slicker dog accustomed to the din of Manhattan.

The day has been long for the Guldstein family. Gerry and Stephanie arranged their beds earlier so they could be comfortable when they finished for the night. Yawning and stretching, they are tempted to go to bed for the evening, but as exhausted as they are, they try to push forward. There is still so much left to do. Nana and Grandpa take turns holding and hugging Hannah before making their excuses to leave.

Nana rarely says she is tired, priding herself on her ability to work like a horse, though recently she has not been as energetic as she once was. Grandpa and Nana owned an upscale dress and accessory store on the east side of Manhattan from the fifties until they took a late retirement a few years ago.

"I worked six days a week, standing on my feet for at least eight hours a day for most of my life," Nana says, explaining her stamina.

By the end of her career, her kvetching about work annoyed Grandpa so much he would insist on closing up shop early.

"No more! Time to close!" Grandpa would say, knowing full well that unless he forced her, Nana would keep working no matter how exhausted she felt.

Then they closed the store and moved away from the hustle of the city, leaving their old brownstone behind.

Grandpa and Nana decided to give Gerry and Steph the rent money from their real estate as a gift to help pay the expenses for their new home in Long Island. There was even enough extra cash to put away for little Hannah. Their generosity has never gone unmentioned, and Stephanie and Gerry have endured listening to the elder Guldsteins boast about their gift *ad nauseam.*

Grandpa and Nana search for their coats, finding them beneath a soiled drop cloth the movers mistakenly left behind. Having to add in her two cents, Nana apologizes for meddling in their business. "Forgive me for making the boxes into such an issue," she says, "but both of you were acting so *meshugena!*"

"C'mon Ma, they're only boxes," Gerry insists.

"Okay, okay. Your father and I are worn out from all the excitement, and besides, we want you to have some time alone on your first night living in the house."

It is so convenient that we live only a few miles away, Nana thinks, walking out the door.

It has been a tiring Christmas Eve, but a memorable one, marking their first night in their new home. Christmas Day will be an occasion to look forward to, not only because of the Wilkersens' invitation, but also because Hannah will be opening her first Hanukkah present when the sun goes down. Stephanie hid her gifts in the master bedroom beside the bed in a large Tupperware container, and covered it with a towel just in case Hannah became too curious. Nana and Grandpa were probably home already. It was not a moment too soon for Gerry and Stephanie, whose patience for listening to his parents talk about how generous they had been to them had waned a long time ago.

Hannah is tucked into her daybed-style crib, custom made with sides and a headboard, and railings that can be removed when she is older. Stephanie often reminisces about her uncle when she puts Hannah down in her bed—he ordered it for her the day she was born. Hannah lies comfortably on her back, surrounded by her stuffed animals, with Gerry and Stephanie nearby to watch over her. They've expected her to fuss in her new room, but she surprises them by falling into a sound sleep.

"Adjusting to the new environment is going to be more difficult for me," Gerry tells Stephanie.

"I seem to be going through it too," she admits.

Leaving the door open, he orders Roger to lie down and stay at the threshold to guard Hannah. "Bark if she wakes up," Gerry tells Roger, who barks once in reply.

Stephanie and Gerry go downstairs to relax and have a glass of wine on the couch together. The menorah Gerry's parents had passed down to them ceremoniously stands on the fireplace ledge. It is time to unwind. As they sip their wine, they laugh about Gerry's mom.

"Watch out, you're not far behind, Steph," Gerry banters.

She slaps his thigh. "I'm not like that, am I?"

The Wilkersens' home is entirely lit up and quite a sight to see as Gerry and Stephanie cuddle in a fluffy throw blanket, with Stephanie's flashlight safely beside her—a habit she picked up at the apartment to spot bugs at night.

"Oh, come on, Steph. We're done with all of that," he cajoles, taking the light from her hand. "You don't need it here," he adds, laughing to lighten her mood.

Stephanie fumbles trying to take the flashlight back, too tired to insist. "Gerry," she says, "they come out at night when it's dark in the house. There may be some hiding."

Gerry holds her hand. Before long they doze off, awakening to find they have slept longer than they intended. Stephanie feels a kink in her neck. Gerry stretches and turns off the lights so they can go up to check on Hannah and Roger and finally go to their bedroom.

When they stand up, they catch sight of the shadow of the Wilkersens' car next to the wall. They stop to watch. Roger barks at the roar of the car, which is unusual for him.

"Quiet!" Gerry calls out in a hushed tone. "You'll wake Hannah!" Roger is up on his feet, peering over the railing at the dark silhouette while nosy Gerry and Stephanie eye their neighbors with the one ounce of strength they have left. They hear faint yaps from Murphy, greeting his family. Theodore Wilkersen Jr. steps inside to get the leash for Murphy's last stroll of the evening.

"Come on, Steph," Gerry says. "Let's get some more sleep before we have to get up. And leave the flashlight on the couch, you don't need it anymore."

She quickly tucks the light under her robe, not suspecting he saw her hide it, though he did.

Once Emma Wilkersen enters her house, she and her daughter go directly to bed, leaving the two Theos to fend for themselves. Emma wants to be rested for her early start in the morning, knowing she will look older if her face shows any signs of fatigue.

Theo Sr. goes into the kitchen for a late-night snack of the special pastries the caterers bake for him every year. He wants them now and can barely wait to taste them. His sweet tooth is seldom satisfied. Emma never hesitates to tell him to control his appetite for desserts, especially his clandestine snacks.

"You eat too much sugar," Emma says. "That's the reason you get headaches and can't sleep."

His son also tells him, "Too much sugar, Dad. You know your age is getting up there. Eat yogurt or fruit like me."

Theo Sr. is irritated at his son's reference to his age. He neither feels old nor looks it.

Theo Jr. comes in from walking Murphy, steps into the kitchen, and chides his father for eating the pastries, cautioning him in a singsong voice, "Mom will be angry when she sees some of them are missing."

"You and your mom are always badgering me," Theo Sr. retorts. "I was thinking that when you strolled in."

Theo Jr. points out to his father that his mom's kitchen is messy. "She's going to kill you, Dad."

Theo Sr. waves off his son. "The kitchen was already messy before I came in, and these were made for me. You should know that by now. And don't concern yourself. I'll clean up. It's the same every year."

"Yeah, I'm sure they are especially for you, and I'm sure Mom said she instructed the caterer not to bake anything for you this year."

"No, she didn't say that."

Theo Sr. leans over to dim the kitchen lights so Emma, his lovely but high-strung wife, won't be able to see him if she peers over the stairwell. Another reprimand would be too vexing.

Theo Jr. steps away with his snack. "Good night, Dad. Enjoy!"

Theo Sr. pours himself a large glass of ice-cold milk, selects six pastries, and places them on the counter. He tastes the first one—it is scrumptious. He shuts his tired eyes, savoring each bite. While licking his lips and hovering his hand above the plate, he decides which one to take next. *Maybe I'll simply eat them all,* he thinks.

Suddenly, he yanks his hand back. "Hey!" he cries out in shock. "What's that? Can't be…a bug? Oh no, there's a beetle in my house!"

He grabs one of Emma's glossy magazines, rolls it tightly in his hands, and thwacks it at the large beetle, but it scuttles away before he can kill it. He grumpily moves his milk and pastries to the table. *How could I miss that damn bug?* he wonders.

Before he can sit, he exclaims, "Oh shoot, there you are!" He jerks away from the table, tilting back the chair so it nearly falls over. He flails his arms in the air in an effort to keep himself upright and manages to succeed in regaining his balance just in time. He spots the beetle scampering across a box with a large cake in it. He pauses, slaps the magazine down once more, and again and again on the marble counter, but the beetle keeps dodging him. Had anyone witnessed his dance with the beetle, they would have surely broken into laughter at his awkward attempts to hit the bug.

He gazes around the kitchen as he drinks his milk and devours his pastries before launching another attack on the elusive insect.

As he stands guard by the table, he notices all the flowers for the party. *That's where the beetle must have come from,* he muses. He sits and relaxes a bit. *I should throw those flowers in the garbage, but Emma would have a fit.*

He finishes his snack, stands, stretches, and yawns, unaware that two other beetles have crossed the counter. *I am too darn exhausted to chase you,* he decides. *Emma and her flowers! It certainly is a shame to bring bugs into the house on Christmas Eve! I will call those florists immediately after Christmas and give them a piece of my mind!*

Leaving the battle zone, Theo Sr. climbs upstairs with a full stomach. He crawls into bed, leaning over Emma to wish her a Merry Christmas, and kisses her gently on the cheek. She smiles and turns over on her side, hugging her pillow and talking to herself. She goes back to sleep, snoring lightly.

All is peaceful now in the Wilkersen house. It was such an entertaining Christmas Eve, and what a great Christmas Day to look forward to tomorrow!

But, as they are sleeping, small invaders are entering their kitchen. The only audible noises are Theo Sr.'s grating snoring and Murphy's whining and occasional soft bark.

Chapter Six

CHRISTMAS DAY AT THE WILKERSENS

The Guldsteins and the Wilkersens all wake up on Christmas Day, pausing for a moment to watch the scant snowflakes drift to the ground. The Guldsteins watch the spectacle longer than the Wilkersens, who are taking showers early, preparing to dress for their holiday party.

Stephanie checks the list she compiled of things to do from A to Z. She is wearing a vintage bathrobe with pom-poms her mother sent her from England. *It is warm and perfect,* Stephanie thinks, *for the winters on Long Island, where it is colder than Manhattan.* She and her mother have a close relationship, so her mother knows her daughter's taste when buying vintage clothing at the secondhand stores Stephanie loves so much.

Gerry admires his wife's talent for decorating

their new home, arranging furniture, and organizing the kitchen, but jokingly dubs her "Ms. Guldstein Number Two, Organizational Queen."

"I'll take that as a compliment," Stephanie sarcastically replies. "Gerr," she asks, "have you seen my crystal water glasses?"

"Why no, I haven't," he says coughing haltingly. "I'm sure they'll turn up."

Roger is walking along with Hannah, taking small steps as she holds onto the fur of his back. Gerry cautions Hannah to be nice to Roger, but she pulls hard on his furry neck anyway. Roger emits an occasional squeal.

Hannah has been awake since early in the morning, talking and laughing. Later in the evening it will be time to tear the wrapping paper from her Hanukkah gift, and she is overly excited by Gerry and Stephanie's enthusiasm for the holiday. Gerry has taken the Tupperware tub of gifts downstairs and is piling Hannah's presents, one for each night of Hanukkah, onto the living room floor.

Happiness fills every inch of the Guldsteins' new home. Nana added to the furor the day before by telling Hannah she could open her gift once the sun went down and the menorah was lit according to Jewish tradition. Hannah now sits in the middle of the mountain of gifts beside Stephanie. Gerry flashes photograph after photograph of the happy home scene. Occasionally, Hannah reaches out and touches the brightly wrapped packages. It's an attraction she cannot resist, and tears the paper on the end of one of her packages—tempted by the idea of opening presents as any child would be, especially a one year old.

Stephanie notices Hannah reaching to rip the paper on another present. "Hannah, those are Hanukkah presents, we only open one of those a night for Hanukkah. It is still daytime, so you mustn't touch."

Hannah looks up at her mother and listens to what she is saying to her, but at the same time, her fingers keep straying back to the brightly colored paper on the gifts.

Among the presents is Roger's box of biscuits from England, an extra-large package he easily sniffs out. He also gets a new tug toy and a scarf, thanks to Nana, embroidered with his telephone number. Anticipating his walk outside, Roger saunters up and down the stairs several times over. Gerry prepares him for their morning walk while Stephanie and Hannah brush their teeth in the upstairs bathroom together.

After dressing Roger in his soft hand-knit sweater and new scarf, Gerry opens the front door and yells upstairs, "Look at the snow falling!"

"Yes, I know," Stephanie answers, "I can see it through the hallway window. It's going to be a Bing Crosby White Christmas for the neighbors!" Which sets off Gerry singing "White Christmas" in his characteristically jarring off-key tone.

"Honey!" Stephanie calls out. "Take Roger out, okay?" Gerry continues to sing while Roger sits with his head cocked to one side, looking puzzled.

Hannah is eager to get back to the living room, where her presents are scattered across the floor. She makes her wishes known by screaming until her face turns bright red and she gasps for air.

Although Gerry and Stephanie didn't find the time to buy and exchange gifts, he did give her cash to shop in her beloved small stores, so she can't wait to scout out the biggest and best sales of the season on Long Island after New Year's.

Remaining patient long enough, Roger finally slips by Gerry through the door, tugging on his leash, pulling his master outside as he tries to put on his hood and gloves. "Slow down, boy. I'm coming," he says, but Roger can't wait any longer.

Gerry thinks back to the time Roger was a pup in the old apartment. He never had an accident except for the one time Gerry ignored his barks and whines to go out because he was on the phone. Gerry recalled how Roger had lowered his ears, crawled underneath the bed and hid, afraid to show his face.

Once outside, Gerry notices that he and Mr. Wilkersen share the same responsibility—walking the dogs in the morning. Murphy is pulling Theo Sr. along, too. Theo Sr. calls out to Gerry, who does not hear him. The wind and light snow muffle Theo Sr.'s voice, and Gerry has his head turned away.

"Hey there, neighbor!" he shouts again. Roger barks. Gerry pivots around.

"Sorry, did you call to me?" he asks.

"Yes, how is your move coming along?"

"We're in the arranging and rearranging stage now. We've moved the furniture in the living room at least a dozen times."

Roger and Murphy get tangled in their leashes as they get acquainted with one another. Both growl warily, each letting the other know that eventually they will be friends.

Theo and Gerry struggle to untangle the two dogs, switching leashes several times as they untangle the dogs from each other. Both dogs watch with slight satisfaction on their faces at being able to get the upper hand over their masters. Finally, after several minutes, they have the leashes straightened out again and are off on their walk.

Theo and Gerry take turns describing their respective evenings: Gerry speaks volumes about the move, and Theo Sr. relates a detailed account of his family's outing in the city. He eventually focuses his conversation on his dinner, recounting it with a lengthy description of his prime rib and dessert. The new neighbors like each other right away.

"Don't forget, you have to come over later," says Theo Sr.

"Sure thing," Gerry responds.

"The party starts at noon with our family and goes on all day and night! And save your appetite; we have so much food!"

"Thanks. We will definitely be there after my mother comes by to babysit for Hannah, and I'll be sure to tell Stephanie to eat lightly."

Gerry waves goodbye, watching Murphy's tail

wag. The men go back inside their houses with their dogs, each feeling grateful for having such a congenial neighbor.

Light-hearted, Gerry whistles a lilting tune as he enters the front door.

Stephanie is thankful he isn't singing.

He wipes Roger's feet with the towel she left in the hallway on a hook, just as she did in the old apartment. Roger doesn't mind—he lifts each paw automatically with no prompts from his master. What Roger detests, however, are the rubber booties Gerry once tried to fit over his paws. They made him walk as though the ground was on fire and he slipped and slid his way the entire walk. It took his best efforts to keep all four feet planted firmly on the ground. The rubber booties made each of his legs want to go a different direction. Roger recalled taking several belly flops on that walk before Gerry realized the rubber booties were just not going to work for poor Roger.

Roger and Gerry head into the kitchen. Gerry feeds him his egg mixed with dried food, and Roger lies down for a quick nap before Hannah appears, wanting to pull his hair and play with him.

Gerry can hardly wait to tell Stephanie about their friendly neighbor, whom he praises endlessly. "He's very cool—not at all as snobbish as I thought he would be. He's okay."

"Honey, I'm so glad you like him," she says as she serves Gerry his breakfast.

"We have a lot in common, even though we

spoke for only a short time. Don't worry, you'll like him too. Not everyone gets friendly that fast."

"That's right, dear, they don't."

At the Wilkersen house, Theo Sr. is enthusiastically telling Emma how much he likes Gerry, fascinated that his new neighbor is a lawyer and his wife a graphic designer who works from home to be with their daughter. "They don't celebrate Christmas, but they'll come over later to join us," Theo Sr. says.

Emma, however, is too preoccupied with the details of the party, as she always is when planning these occasions, to pay much attention to her husband. She peppers the conversation with perfunctory "Yes, dears." Theo goes on and on anyway. He tags after his wife while she bustles about the house, glancing into every mirror she passes. Every time she stops to inspect her face, she pouts in front of the mirror. Needing constant reassurance of her beauty, Emma repeatedly asks her husband, "How do I look, Theo dear?"

Murphy is in the kitchen, munching on leftover meat and sliced apples for his breakfast. He crunches the apples in the most annoying way while steadfastly guarding his Christmas Eve bone for afterwards.

Theo Jr. is sitting at the table texting his friend in Florida about the chicks in South Beach. "I wish I was there," he writes. His friend sends him shots of his day on the beach, playing Frisbee with bikini-clad beauties.

Jennifer is speaking on the phone to a friend of hers about what time she should come to the party. "Six p.m., after all the gifts are opened and our family is less stressed," she tells her. She reveals to her friend that her mother is constantly looking in the mirror. She is always fixing her lipstick and hair, then checking her jewelry to make sure it is just enough to complement her dress.

"She has to shine like a movie star," she says. Jennifer's friend can certainly relate to this, as both of their moms are the same way—Long Island beauties.

In fact, all of Jennifer's closest friends say they've never seen Emma looking any way but great. "Mrs. W. is one of the prettiest," they would remark. Even the people in town know Emma is always dressed to kill, making a fashion statement wherever she goes.

Jennifer ends her call, and extends her leg to push away Murphy with her foot. "Oh, c'mon, Mom, you look just fine," Jennifer tells her. "You're not getting ready for the red carpet…although you look it."

Emma puts her nose in the air and shoots a snooty look at Jennifer. Although Jennifer wants to ask her mother a question, it is impossible for her to attract Emma's attention even for a moment, as she is so driven to make herself and her home as perfect as the photographs in her magazines—perhaps too perfect.

Her daughter has unconsciously picked up some of Emma's ways. "Out, Murphy. Go!" Jennifer snaps at her dog, as her mom often does. Murphy looks quizzical.

Emma strives to be a model wife. Perfection means living in her model home and being model perfect herself in every way. She constantly speaks about getting plastic surgery. She is determined to be like Joan Rivers and look younger and younger. Theo Sr. likes to rib her saying, "Well, you may want to look as good as Joan Rivers, but you'll never be that funny!" Her husband's words go unheard whenever he tries to dissuade her from going to such extremes, telling her every part of her is beautiful.

"I love you the way you are," he insists repeatedly. "I don't want a new Emma. It's ridiculous to get so dressed up in our own home. Next thing I know, you'll be asking me to install a runway for you. Let's just be more casual and comfortable."

It seems that the more money Theo Sr. makes, the further Emma's parties stray from the real meaning of Christmas. From year to year the friends and family they host are becoming more plastic as well. They compete with one another. They flaunt their couture fashions and jewelry. Only the most impressive designer names will touch their skin. When the female guests arrive, they greet each other by kissing the air rather than the cheek. This is to make certain not to smudge their perfectly applied makeup, particularly the lipstick. Even when they eat, they carefully tuck the bite-sized morsels inside their mouths so their lips won't touch the food.

The Wilkersens are extravagant. Their maid

works daily to maintain Emma's standards of cleanliness. They hire limousine drivers, a chef, gardeners, pool boys, and snow removal experts. The one chore reserved for Jennifer and Theo Jr. is to take out the trash. Uncle Bob always says, "Heaven forbid they do more and have real chores." ("Heaven forbid" is the expression Uncle Bob uses whenever he is being sarcastic about the family, and the general consensus is that he has worn it out.)

The Wilkersens have three refrigerators in their house, all full and ready for dinner and cocktail party guests throughout the year. Boxes of cakes and pastries cover the counters. In the dining room the buffet tables are lined with silver serving dishes. Two catering companies will help set up the food for the Christmas party, and one will remain to pass out the *hors d'oeuvres* to the guests.

Emma tastefully dons her beautiful designer evening dress, looking fit to be a Miss America Pageant contestant. Murphy sports a handmade scarf with jingle bells that drive Theo Sr. to distraction. "Please, Emma," he begs, "take that off Murphy. The guests will be driven crazy." Emma ignores him.

Theo Sr. goes into the kitchen to make sure the beetle isn't in sight. He hasn't mentioned it to Emma. No way will he tell her about bugs from the flowers, that would send her over the edge. (He did write a note to himself to call an exterminator, and then hid it inside his wallet.) Though their gardeners have always sprayed outside for ants in the summer, the Wilkersens have never once had bugs, not even around the pool. The one Theo Sr. spotted in the kitchen was enormous, almost as large as a newborn infant's fist. *Perhaps it is a rare beetle,* he thinks. He suggests to Emma that she buy fewer flowers next year, but her response is to lift her hand in the air and wave him off. "Oh Theo, please. I will not have a house without flowers!" Theo Sr. removes himself from earshot of Emma's complaining. He sits down in front of the living room's flat-screen TV to watch a news bulletin about a major snowstorm in the city. The police are making automated telephone calls warning residents to stay indoors.

"Should we call the guests, Emma?"

"No. Nothing will ruin my party and it will not be canceled!" Emma's way of dealing with stress is to stop listening if she is about to hear unsettling news.

The snow is falling heavily. At least twelve inches are forecast, maybe more. Emma is peering out the kitchen window at the snow.

"All our guests will arrive before the storm gets worse, and we'll be safely inside," she says, then notices something unsightly in the yard.

"Theo, come over here, quickly!" He runs to her, and she points toward the yard. "What are those boxes leaning against our fence? Who would have done that? We have company on the way, and they detract from the beauty of our yard!"

"Yard? There is no yard—this is winter! Where is the grass?"

"Don't even try to be funny," she retorts, defiantly placing her hands on her hips.

"All I can see is old snow with new snow collecting on top of it," Theo Sr. responds. "Oh Emma, the trash will be hauled away in two days. Stop freaking out! My dear, it's virtually impossible to see the yard, and who would look?"

"Why don't they put those ugly boxes in their garage or crush them into their barrels?" Emma asks in a more modulated tone.

"Why, Emma? It's cold outside, and they are probably tired. What would you like me to do?"

"Well, don't simply stand there. Think of something!"

"It's Christmas, Emma. Let's not dwell on the boxes."

"Well, if you'd like me to stop bothering you, why don't you call someone to take them away or go next door and inform your new friend that he should move them out of sight? We wouldn't trash our yard or their yard for all the neighbors to see, especially on Christmas Day!"

"No, dear, that is not the right thing to do."

"It's Christmas, I know, dear."

"Besides, the snow should cover the boxes before anyone arrives. Be patient, please!" Theo Sr. is not about to stir up the neighbors on Christmas Day, even though they celebrate a different holiday. "It can wait," he whispers to himself.

"I heard that!" Emma shouts suddenly. "Theo, what if one of our guests sees them? Do you know how embarrassed I'll be?"

At a loss for words, he finally says, "Darling, I know how embarrassed you would be, but I don't expect that any of our friends or family will be standing at the sink washing dishes, and they won't be hanging out in the atrium on a stormy day, so who do you think will be looking at those boxes? Tell me, who?"

"Anyone might see out the back windows! Aunt Mary and Aunt Tilly are nosy enough…." Emma is livid, though the boxes are barely noticeable, obscured by the snow except for the corners. Theo Sr. notices Emma's face twitch slightly as she leaves the room.

He is all too familiar with his wife's attitudes. He recalls a time when Emma wasn't quite as spoiled, earlier in their marriage, when she was less acerbic and sweeter. Though he does enjoy dressing up when they go out or for special occasions, Theo Sr. wants to live a less formal daily life the way he and Emma used to, comfortable, without airs.

Those were the best holidays, too, he recalls, getting up early Christmas morning, opening presents with our pajamas on, one or two well-thought-out gifts, never expensive, home-cooked meals and friends. Now everything bothers her. I love a beautiful house, but not if Emma is not herself. She is always worrying about what others think all the time and keeping up with every new thing that comes along. She always has to own the best, only the best.

Theo applies pressure to his brow. He thinks, "How I wish I could turn back the hands of time."

His attention wanders to the cookies on the counter. He tastes one. This is what Christmas is about: food, family, happiness, and no stress. But now Emma is so stressed by Christmas preparations, she loses control of herself and breaks out in hives.

He decides to make her favorite breakfast—a cinnamon bun with an egg. That will take her mind off the boxes and relax her, he thinks. Maybe pour just enough cognac into her coffee to keep her mellow. Emma rarely misses breakfast, though she would starve for the rest of the day to keep her figure.

Murphy prances into the kitchen with his bells jingling as he smells the aroma of the heated bun. He knows Emma will give him just a pinch of her food.

"Emma, where are you?" Theo Sr. calls out.

"I'm here in the den," she replies in a softer tone, though still upset.

As Theo Sr. wanders from room to room on the way to his wife, he can't help noticing how exquisite the decorated estates are in the décor magazines that she has carefully placed on her lovely tables. But everywhere he looks appears just as untouchable and impersonal as the glossy pages. Emma's home clearly showcases her decorating expertise, and dressing the house for the holidays is one of her yearly projects.

He truly appreciates his wife's talents. Before selling her business in New York, she was one of the city's top interior decorators. She has fashioned

Theo Jr.'s bedroom into a sports haven. Emma embellished Jennifer's room with a modern palette of various shades of pink, orange, and lime green, with white shabby chic furniture. She chose the leopard and zebra pillows as her signature touch.

The Wilkersens' master bedroom suite is a dramatic retreat with a classic limestone fireplace, floor to ceiling sheer silk drapes with tassels, and thick, ornate crown moldings. Their bedroom fixtures are from France and create the ambience of a French chateau. The attached double-vanity bathroom boasts doors of clear glass and chrome, etched by a famous glass artist—fit for a king and queen. The white porcelain tub has chrome fixtures with knobs of the same porcelain. Gray and white art deco tile work furnishes the finishing touch.

Theo Sr.'s home office is on its own level across from the media room and bar. As an investment banker, he often travels abroad, so his office is enriched with exotic collectibles from all over the world, locked in custom mahogany wall cases with leaded glass.

Most are gifts from colleagues and clients. He appreciates the pieces for their artistic value, particularly one of his favorites, an owl of rough-cut stone with an onyx beak and amber stone eyes. His prize possession is a set of old, exotic elephant tusks. He also displays a collection of bar bottles from the 1920s and 1930s, with little space left to acquire more of them. *Soon I'll need to add a wing to the house just for my collections*, he thinks.

Emma smiles when her husband places the breakfast tray in front of her. "Better now, dear?" he asks, seeing that his wife's expression has relaxed and she appears more content. He is relieved she has forgotten about the cartons, or so it seems.

"Theo, please make certain that everything is going as it should. It's almost noon, and everyone will be coming soon."

"Drink your coffee, dear," he blithely suggests.

"I appreciate your making breakfast for me, my dear husband, but don't think for a moment I've forgotten about those boxes!"

Shaken and dismayed by this, he watches her sip her coffee, wishing she would guzzle the cup down. Emma hands Theo her empty plate. He is so familiar with his wife's ways that he should have known she would remember.

Once back in the kitchen, Theo Sr. grumbles as he rinses the dishes. As he turns away from the sink for one split second, he spots the sly beetle out of the corner of his eye. It is scurrying from one shadow to the next across the counter, where all the cakes and pastries are set out for the guests.

That bug better not run over the pastries, he thinks, *I refuse to trash them.* Having only a few moments before the doorbell rings, he rolls up the same magazine and poses it to crush the unsuspecting bug.

Smack! He misses. "What?" he blurts out and tries again. Smack! Smack! He is flustered by the sheer speed of the beetle.

Smack! He has flattened some croissants on a

tray that were ready to go out on the table. "Oh, dang!"

He covers the crushed pastries with a dishtowel, and then hides the ruined tray underneath another one, hoping it won't be noticed. No one will know he crushed them; rather, they would think, the tray on the top flattened the delicacies.

"This is Christmas," Theo says to the bug, "and you are not going to be part of the celebration!"

Afraid Emma will catch him hunting down the critter, he shifts the platters around delicately. He looks behind everything, and then sees the slightest of movements.

"There you are!" he mutters as he spies the beetle tucked behind a tray. Infuriated, he thumps the magazine down on top of the beetle, but the magazine strikes the edge of the tray and the pastries go flying in every direction. He catches as many of them as he can. Theo is now standing there in the middle of the kitchen, with his hands stuffed with pastries, and they are beginning to crumble ever so slightly from the pressure of his hands. He is intent on putting them onto an unoccupied tray.

Meanwhile, unseen by Theo, the bug ventures out at the far end of the long counter.

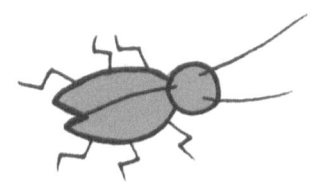

"Gotcha!" he says as he inspects the magazine for the remains of the bug, finding none. "How can this be?" he frets. He spots the bug again, darts to where his prey stands, and... Smack! Smack! Smack! "Just once more and you are mine!"

He can't believe the resilience of that bug. Sweat beads on his forehead, and he imagines what Emma would say if she saw him. She would tell him to change his shirt, that's all. He has to relax.

"Dad, what are you doing with Mom's magazine? She'll kill you!" squeaks Jennifer, who has just entered the kitchen behind her father's back.

He hesitates, and thinking fast, he says, "I was thumbing through it, looking at the pictures!"

"Really? With the magazine all rolled up? Okay, Dad," she says, her tone expressing her skepticism.

His explanation doesn't satisfy her. "Later, Dad," she says as her phone rings again and she answers, speaking in an animated way to her friend.

Theo Sr. is relieved his daughter has better things to do and was not more curious as she left the kitchen. He puts the magazine down, thoroughly frustrated by his crawling adversary. He makes certain to lay the magazine at the bottom of a stack of decorating catalogues to flatten it out so his wife won't suspect.

Victorious, the beetle is still lurking somewhere in the kitchen. Theo Sr. hopes the beetle stays where it is, close to the bouquets and flowering plants. He must try to keep Emma out of the kitchen as much as possible.

The Wilkersen household is ready and waiting for the guests to arrive. They haven't opened their presents yet. Theo Jr. and Jennifer made it known long before Christmas that they wanted electronics. Theo Jr. also requested anything related to sports, especially if season tickets were involved. Jennifer demanded clothes and a new iPod.

Emma reminds them to be patient and that they will be opening their presents after their aunts, uncles, and cousins arrive. Theo Jr. is excited about the present he arranged and bought for his mother. Who wouldn't love a weeklong trip to a spa where she'll be able to relax and be pampered without makeup or worrying about what to wear? It is a surprise he is planning to give her after the other guests leave.

Theo Sr.'s fascination with westerns inspired Jennifer to book a weekend stay on a ranch in Texas with horseback riding and a mystery western theme. She knows her dad will be thrilled.

All of the uncles and aunts, except for Aunt Eve, give Jennifer and Theo Jr. money for the holidays. The children always look forward to receiving their envelopes, knowing full well that the amount of money always increases with their age. Everyone gives ten dollars for each year until they're twenty-five.

Aunt Eve, a real Yankee from New England, gives each of them a vintage Red Sox postcard every year, and probably will until the day she dies. She is a self-made millionaire at ninety. She is a woman who invested well and who lived alone her entire life in a modest Nantucket home. She comes to New York City to her apartment for the holidays. The family says her frugality borders on meanness. She has never spent her money on anyone else, nor does she spend it on herself. That is the reason she remains as rich as she is, according to Uncle Bob, who seems to have an opinion on everyone and everything.

Jennifer admires and loves her aunt because she is unlike any other woman she has met and is so knowledgeable. Aunt Eve gave Jennifer the diary she wrote when she was a young girl to keep until her death, when Jennifer will be given the key to her aunt's old, locked book.

Time is passing slowly, or so it seems. Large snowflakes are falling silently, and the fireplaces are lit and roaring. This is the first time all day the family is sitting on the couch together, enjoying the few calm moments they have before the doorbell begins to ring.

While Theo Sr. relaxes with his arm around Emma, he daydreams about how wonderful it would be having a Christmas without guests. Just this once, it would be wonderful to have a peaceful holiday by themselves just like in old times. *Just once without presents or guests,* he thinks, *but Emma loves socializing.*

Emma is thinking about her gift to Theo. She purchased an authentic pair of western boots and a cowboy hat for him to wear on his trip to Texas.

When Jennifer informed Emma about her present to her dad, Emma promised Jennifer they would go shopping during Theo Sr.'s weekend away. Emma is sure her husband will be pleased with his gifts, and for the first time in years, Emma, Theo Sr., and the kids are on the same page.

Emma offers to make coffee, tea, or cocoa, but no one except her wants any. "I am going into the kitchen to make a hot cup of tea, so let me know if you change your minds," she tells them.

"No, no dear, sit down," says Theo Sr., standing up abruptly. "I'll bring you some tea, or do you want another cup of coffee?"

They all glance at each other and break out in laughter at the same time. The very idea of their father making tea was unthinkable unless it was for a special occasion or plastic surgery. The children, even Emma herself, are in the habit of getting their own drinks.

"Mom, I told you that Dad was behaving strangely," Jennifer says, laughing so hard she choked. "First reading Mom's decorating magazine, and now making tea. Really? Are you sure you're feeling okay Dad? Maybe you should sit for a while."

"You were reading my magazines, Theo? You've never even picked one up before. Are you okay?"

"Emma, why don't you stay to answer the door while I make tea? I don't feel like greeting guests quite yet. I won't be more than a minute."

"You're acting strangely. Did you have too much to drink, Theo? Are you ill?" Emma questioned with actual concern in her voice.

"No, dear, I'm not sick! It's Christmas! Christmas!"

"Maybe he did have too much to drink," Jennifer suggests.

The truth is he doesn't want to take the chance of his wife seeing the beetle. He thinks he has been clever by offering to make the tea and seems not to notice that he has not been successful at convincing anyone. With that illusion in his mind, he hurries off to the kitchen.

You're up to something, Theo, Emma thinks to herself.

The doorbell abruptly chimes—DING-DONG, DING-DONG, DING! Company has arrived. The tea will have to wait until another time, though Theo did manage to squeeze in one brief moment to check for bugs. None are in clear sight.

Murphy jingles as he approaches the front door, adding an enthusiastic "Woof, woof, woof!" to the lively scene. The party is about to begin.

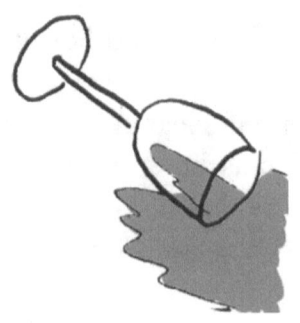

Chapter Seven

FAMILY AND FRIENDS ARRIVE

The clang of the loud chimes causes Murphy to bark madly. Doorbells, vacuums, rock-and-roll—all are threatening to him. It's a wonder the bells around his neck don't drive him mad.

"Quiet!" Jennifer shouts. "Didn't you tell everyone to let themselves in, Mom?"

"No, Jen, I completely forgot. Try to calm Murphy down."

"You'd think they would know by now," Jennifer says under her breath. "They're adults."

More often than not, Emma would instruct her friends to call when they were in front of the house. "Don't ring the bell!" she would tell them. But Aunt Tilly never follows orders anyway.

Her toy poodle, Pookie, is Murphy's nemesis, and he could smell them outside the door. Murphy doesn't appreciate other dogs entering his territory, and he senses something odd about Aunt Tilly and Pookie whenever they visit.

Murphy isn't the only one bothered by them, however. Neither of the Theos can tolerate them either. Pink annoys them, and they find Aunt Tilly's obsession with the color obnoxious. She dresses Pookie in pink because, she says, "All female poodles should be in pink."

But Aunt Tilly isn't a poodle, Theo Sr. thinks, *why does she dress in pink?* Her glasses have pink frames. Her fingernails and toenails are painted pink. Her dress and pocketbook are pink. Her lipstick and coats are pink. Whenever Pookie comes to visit, Theo Jr. rolls his eyes. When he was younger, he asked her why both she and Pookie were dressed identically, and Aunt Tilly's response wasn't particularly informative. "Just because, my dear," was all she replied. "Just because."

Aunt Tilly carries out her dictum about poodles in pink down to the smallest detail, painting Pookie's claws a bright fuchsia to offset the sugar-candy pink of her ear bows and outfits. If she could, Aunt Tilly would dye Pookie's fur pink, as well as her own hair, but her husband Arnold has warned her not to, or she and her poodle will be visiting, not living, in any house where he is. He frightens her to tears—and surprisingly they are not pink tears. He despises the color and removed the pink pillows she put in the back seat of the car for Pookie to sit on. Instead, he threw his gym towel there and ordered Pookie to lie down. It irks him that the interior of their home is painted in different shades of pink. Tilly knows her husband means what he says, and she doesn't dare cross that line.

As Aunt Tilly and Pookie wait at the front door, Murphy smells them and barks uncontrollably, to the point where Theo Sr. threatens to muzzle him.

"Don't you dare do that to our Murphy!" Emma suddenly snaps. "Jennifer, what did I tell you? Keep him quiet! Take Murphy to your room and keep him there until all the guests arrive!"

"Yes, Mommy dearest," she says. She complains that she is always the one who has to take Murphy.

"I heard you, Jennifer. After Pookie stops shaking, you can bring him back."

"Okay, Mom, but it's not fair," she replies. "Why does the 'pink pain' have to come with Aunt Tilly? She could get a sitter. C'mon, Murph!"

Jennifer stops whining once she realizes Murphy has given her an excuse for going upstairs to text her friends rather than opening the door for the guests and having to wear her best silicone smile.

If Jennifer could have her way, the family would be away on a warm, sunny island for Christmas. Theo Jr. and Jennifer can hardly wait for New Year's. That is when they'll be having fun far away from the cold. Jennifer is looking forward to catching the sun's rays and watching the handsome guys and lifeguards. Theo can't wait to watch all the girls in bikinis compete with one another.

Murphy wags his tail. Usually the housekeeper

feeds him human food every day, and he sniffs the air, expecting to be fed. As Jennifer sends an e-mail and then looks in the mirror, pouting, shaking her head from side to side to arrange her long hair, Murphy gazes at her in the same way his eyes follow Emma when she is in front of a mirror. Though not aware of it, Jennifer is becoming more like her mother every day. She has become vain and snobbish, a mirror image of her mother.

Next door, the Guldsteins are forever positioning their furniture and hanging pictures on the walls when they notice the crowd of people emerging from their cars at the Wilkersens' home. "Honey, look at how many people are arriving all dressed up!" Gerry remarks. Hard as it is to see the guests clearly through the screen of thick, white snowflakes, the fashion show is truly about to begin.

"I'm looking forward to going over there," Gerry tells Stephanie. "And I don't think you should worry about what to wear. The smell of their food is making me hungry."

"Me too," she says. "They look like they're going to a ball, don't they, Gerr?"

"It's nearly impossible to see clearly with the snow blowing. We don't have to overdress," he tells Stephanie, who is relieved because she doesn't want to search for her party clothes. The vintage clothing in her wardrobe consists of one-of-a-kind dresses, and even her shoes and accessories are second to none.

Back at the Wilkersens, Emma is putting a huge

platter of filet mignon with shallots, ginger, and jumbo grilled shrimp into one of their ovens to heat them slightly. In the lower oven are stuffed mushrooms in wine sauce with chicken thighs and orange peel.

Theo Sr. peers around the kitchen doorway, scrutinizing the counters, making certain a beetle isn't lurking about. He stays close to the kitchen, checking in with Emma to see if she needs help, but she shoos him away. *Thank heaven,* she thinks. *He's gone.*

Then he goes to his favorite spot in the house during the holidays: his custom-made leather and glass-top bar. The old movie photos under the glass create a picture-perfect atmosphere for having a drink. Hanging on his chocolate brown walls are images of movie memorabilia, most of them signed. The picture frames are painted in brilliant reds, oranges, and bright white—colors that pop out, giving the bar area the appearance of a theater.

Theo Sr. may feel tired of entertaining guests every single Christmas, but he genuinely enjoys family gatherings. Over the years he has perfected rum drinks with crushed fruit, proudly mixed at his prized bar. Most of the bar guests hold a glass in one hand while selecting *hors d'oeuvres* from the server. The Polish sausages wrapped in a cinnamon flaky crust are garnished with bay and mint leaves, and are so much in demand the servers carry tray after tray throughout the house. Emma has scheduled two servers, even though Theo Sr. said he wanted only one. Emma texts him that she wants more servers to come immediately. He texts her back in all uppercase letters: "NO, I DON'T WANT MORE SERVERS IN THE HOUSE. BESIDES, NO ONE WILL COME BECAUSE OF THE POOR DRIVING CONDITIONS." Emma does agree with this, realizing it would be impossible for the caterers to send out more help.

With the exception of the cakes, the guests always finish the food, often taking several helpings because it tastes so good. Even Emma's closest friends have revealed that they "starved for days" so they could eat at her party, and guests who rarely drank sipped Theo's Sr.'s sumptuous rum concoctions.

The nuts and chocolates set out on the bar are imported from several countries, and the coconut chunks are served in bowls made from actual coconuts. Theo Jr. navigates from tray to tray before anyone else can get to them, collecting handfuls of *hors d'oeuvres* to share with Jennifer.

Pookie calms herself down and is content after Aunt Tilly feeds the coddled pink poodle a wide variety of food meant for the human guests, including shrimp and lobster.

Emma calls to Theo Jr. to go upstairs to his sister's room to free Jennifer and Murphy so they can enjoy the food as well. Murphy especially enjoys the food, as his appetite for shrimp is remarkable for a dog. Emma warns Jennifer not to overfeed him shrimp because it makes his breath smell fishy for days.

The number of guests arriving is dwindling, and Theo Jr. and Jennifer's friends will be showing up soon, after 6 p.m. The gifts are now scheduled to be exchanged among the family first, then with their friends. Slightly over fifty people are eating dinner, sitting anywhere they choose in the large house, even around the pool, where there are benches and glass-topped tables and a ceiling heater blowing warm air into the room—an ideal place to see the snow falling through the windows framing the room.

Meanwhile, Gerry and Stephanie are still at work in their house, moving den couches back and forth, and office items from one room to another until Gerry finally decides to use the basement as an office.

Their plan is to dress for the party once Gerry's mom and dad come over to look after Hannah and Roger.

Stephanie jokes with him about how, when they return from the Christmas party, their house will be more organized and cleaner than when they left it. Nana's habit of cleaning exactly where Stephanie has cleaned already was unnerving to Stephanie.

Both Gerry and Stephanie are exhausted from their move and look forward to a pleasant and relaxing house party.

During the days after Christmas there will be more time to relax and sleep. It is a blessing Gerry's job doesn't begin until after New Year's. He is equally thankful they no longer live in the city.

There, it was so easy for Stephanie to rush out to all the after-Christmas sales, while Gerry was forced to babysit.

His mother constantly reminds him that Stephanie buys items only on sale, not at full price, so babysitting is the price he has to pay while Stephanie is out hunting for bargains. Gerry, however, quite enjoys his time alone with his daughter and considers sitting for Hannah a pleasure.

Murphy's tail is wagging vigorously as he stands close to Jennifer's leg. He knows she is getting something for him to eat.

"What is on your tail, boy?" Jennifer asks. "Is it chocolate?" Murphy wags his tail even faster, and the dark spot disappears. She examines his tail closer. "That's strange," she says. "Where did the chocolate go?" Not yet aware of the bugs in the house, she thought something had innocently gotten stuck in his fur. Murphy thinks he has done something wrong and stops wagging his tail.

As Jennifer emerges from the kitchen, aunts and uncles standing nearby tell her how pretty she is and how she has grown into quite a young woman. She is flattered, if not a bit self-conscious. She has indeed blossomed during the past year, but not without help from her mother. Emma advised her to streak her hair blonde and took her to Victoria's Secret to shop for padded bras that accentuate her chest like the ones her friends wear.

Jennifer takes some shrimp for Murphy and

waves her hand behind her back, where Murphy grabs the shrimp, and swallows it greedily. Then he runs his tongue over his chops, eyeing her for more. Jennifer, remembering her mother's warning about not to feed him too much shrimp, gives him a few pieces of steak instead and then kneels down and ruffles the scruff of his neck.

"That's enough for now, boy," she tells him. "Everyone will give you a bite, and Mom and Dad will feed you later. So for now be gone, and don't try to sample any of Mom's cakes!"

Murphy sneezes, satisfied with his intake for now, though the sweet aroma of lobster draws him in. If Murphy is thinking anything, it is, *Why did the pink puff get lobster, and not me? It's my house!*

He sniffs his way about the house, following the scent of the lobster. He intends to sit by a person with lobster on his plate until he is fed, but can't seem to locate any. He walks very cautiously toward the dining room, then the living room, as if hunting down prey in slow motion. He finds vivacious Emma in a small circle of guests, telling a story with an animated expression on her face and gesturing with her hands. He nuzzles up to her side, whining for more food, but her hands are empty. Discouraged, he bows his head and steps away.

Uncle Bob, noticing Murphy's disappointment, calls him to come, then gives him a morsel of steak and a piece of lobster. Yes, that's it! He rolls over, and Uncle Bob tosses him another chunk of lobster. Murphy barks. Uncle Bob gets down on one knee and gives Murphy a robust hug. "Now go," he says. "You've had enough."

Murphy is careful to avoid Emma, knowing not to upset her during the party, or out he goes. If she sees dog hair anywhere, particularly on her clothes, she'll have a fit.

Murphy deliberately walks up to Pookie, testing to see whether she'll start trembling at his approach. Just as he expected, the pink poodle shivers. Murphy raises his chin to appear to have his nose in the air.

Accomplishing his goal of irritating the pink poodle, he is set on being fed more from the guests' plates. He sits, lifts his paws into begging position, and waves them to and fro, jingling his bells. Emma's friends take out their cameras and snap photos of him. "Good boy," Emma says. Feeling generous, she feeds him some treats. Murphy barks and she gives him more.

Then he lies down directly in front of Aunt Tilly, who tries to shoo him away as she sneezes, acting as if she were allergic to him. Every year it's the same scenario: Aunt Tilly is sitting in Murphy's spot. "He's going to sleep," Emma tells her. "You can move to that empty chair." But that does not deter Aunt Tilly, who puts her nose in the air and moves just a few inches away from Murphy, as if he carried some dreadful disease. She is not going to the other side of the room to satisfy this dog!

Opening one eye, Murphy sees his trick worked—Aunt Tilly has moved from directly in front of the fireplace. Though she hasn't budged more than a few inches, at least it is not he who was inconvenienced. This disturbs her. She prefers being closer to the warm fire, but Murphy isn't about to let that happen.

He sprawls out. With both eyes shut, Murphy sniffs the food, and his nose moves up and down ever so slightly. Emma glances at him. Unaware that several others have already given him food, she assumes he is waiting to be fed. After filling a small bowl with steak, she places it in front of him. His tail wags briskly. It hits Aunt Tilly's legs with each wag. Murphy is taking the opportunity to put a little more effort into his tail wagging than he normally does. "You're such a good dog," Emma coos.

Pookie comes to a stand in Aunt Tilly's lap, staring at Murphy with his bowlful. Murphy looks up, baring his teeth. Pookie retreats to a corner of the sofa and crouches there, trembling at Aunt Tilly's side. Murphy watches her fuss over Pookie as he continues eating: "Oh, my poor baby, did that bad dog frighten you?"

Murphy gulps down the last of his steak, and turns to look at Pookie, still trembling in the corner of the couch. Murphy barks at Pookie, saying, "You little pink powder puff, what gives you the right to sit on my couch; and your master, she always takes my place, just to upset my routine. If you had an ounce of intelligence, you would get her to move across the room, before I make you into a tasty pink pastry and eat you up in one gulp."

Pookie understood Murphy completely. In her high pitched yap, she said, "My master does what she wants. She likes to sit by the fire; you are an ill-mannered mutt, otherwise you would have let her sit there." She continued to yap. "You know she would feed me shrimp and lobster all day long if I wanted it. She gives me anything that I want. Can you say that, you big mutt?" questioned Pookie.

Murphy smiled widely and said, "As a matter of fact, lots of people will give me anything I want. Look at the big bowl of steak that she gave me. I didn't see anyone giving you that much steak. In fact, you just watch me, and I'll show you how good I am at getting what I want."

Murphy started to work his way around the room. He stopped at Uncle Bob, his previous benefactor, who had a plate filled with shrimp and lobster. Murphy put his head on Uncle Bob's knee and whimpered ever so slightly, flashing his big puppy dog eyes. Uncle Bob looked down at him and gave him a piece of lobster, which Murphy swallowed down promptly. Once again, he put his head on Uncle Bob's knee and gave a quiet little whimper. This time, Murphy actually managed to get a tear to run down his face when he whimpered. Uncle Bob could not bear to hear him cry. He said, "You know Murphy, I think I took more than I can handle. How about you finish off this plate for me?" Then Uncle Bob put the plate down on the floor in front of Murphy. Murphy started to eat slowly, savoring every bite.

He stopped for one moment, glanced over his shoulder and gave Pookie a gloating look that made her burst out into non-stop yapping, which Aunt Tilly could not control. Finally, Aunt Tilly lifted her body out of the comfort of the couch and moved across the room, still holding tightly to Pookie. Once they were seated there, she scolded Pookie, and the yapping stopped for the rest of the night.

Meanwhile, Murphy went back to devouring his huge plate of shrimp and lobster.

Jennifer, who is standing nearby, overhears what her aunt had said earlier and sticks her fingers down her throat. "I could just puke," she tells her brother.

The party is getting livelier and louder. The best Bose stereo system money can buy is wired into every room, filling the air with classic movie tracks and Christmas music.

"Look at Uncle Jeff!" Theo Jr. points out. Uncle Jeff is swaying from side to side, singing along with the music, but with the words and melody from another song.

"I think he's had enough eggnog to drink!" remarks Theo Jr. "He's tripping!"

"Ya think?" inquires his sister, giggling unstoppably. "C'mon Theo," she says, "let's get some eggnog. Dad won't see us!"

"Join us for a minute, honey!" Emma calls upstairs to Theo Sr., and then turns to her children. "You join us too, my dears!"

"Okay, Mom, I'll get Dad and we'll be right there!" Theo Jr. yells out, but instead heads for where Jennifer is.

The guests' noise is so raucous it drowns out the music. Jennifer saunters over to the bar and, as unobtrusively as she can, fills two large kitchen glasses with eggnog, then the clear rum drink so her mother won't suspect she spiked the eggnog. Emma passes the bar as she goes toward the stairs to look for Theo Sr. at precisely the moment Jennifer is pouring the drinks. She doesn't know Theo Jr. is with Jennifer as she approaches the bar.

"What are you both doing?" she asks her daughter.

"Getting ice for our eggnogs," Jennifer quickly replies. "We're using the everyday glasses so our drinks won't get confused."

"What a good idea! Your father and I don't want you drinking the rum."

"No problem," Jennifer reassures her.

Mellower than usual, Emma doesn't question her daughter's actions. "Come join us," Emma says.

Jennifer signals to Theo Jr. to be cool. "Let's get hammered," she says.

"OK," he replies. "Mom's getting way tipsy, and so is Dad. They'll never notice!"

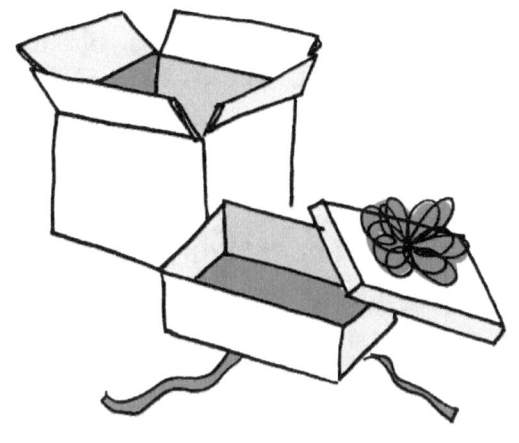

Chapter Eight

OPENING THE GIFTS

Theo Sr. makes an announcement: "Quiet down, quiet down, please! It's time to take a seat and open our gifts!"

Everyone is beginning to feel a little too happy and doesn't care what anyone else is saying as Uncle Bob makes a toast, then another, to "good cheer." The only ones listening are Murphy and Pookie.

While the humans assemble themselves, a small army of creeping, crawling bugs is marching in the dining room, invading the platters of vegetables and the ornate silver dishes of roast beef—stealthily, silent, and unseen. The servers are circulating among the guests, who reach for the trays from their various positions.

Theo Sr.'s deep voice sounds blustery as he speaks into the microphone, "Let's open the gifts!"

As they lift their glasses to toast again, Murphy and Pookie join forces to clean whatever crumbs are on the floor, undeterred by the critters running past them. Murphy is on one side of the sofa, and Pookie is on the other, close but not too close—Murphy partially shows his teeth from time to time to keep the pink poodle in her place.

The rest of the guests drift into the grand living room, where they gather near the tree. Some adults sit on the Brazilian hardwood floor with the children, while others stand or take seats on the sofas, chairs, and tasseled ottomans. The plush area rugs are so thick no one minds sitting on them.

Everything is proceeding as planned. Both family and close friends brought big gift boxes, and everyone hushes with caution, in anticipation of exchanging them, as they do every year. Cameras flash every few seconds.

As the gifts are passed out, the chatter in the room turns into gossip about who bought whom what in past years, who wore what, and who went where. This occurs year in and year out. It is the "same old, same old."

One of the younger children points to the snow outside the window and yells, "Can we go out?" The other nieces and nephews gather at the window, pressing their noses against the panes of glass. "Yes, please, can we?" They beg and nag to go outside with such urgency that Theo Sr. has to put his foot down—"No presents if you go out." The children resume sitting immediately.

The large, wet flakes appear surreal. "Look, it's a blizzard, Auntie Emma!" Andy exclaims.

"Yes, dear, it is," she replies.

"The weather forecast predicted five to ten inches more," Aunt Mary adds.

"I heard maybe a foot or more!" interjects Aunt Tilly. "That's much too deep for the little ones. You heard your Uncle Theo."

"Hope you have enough blankets, Emma," Aunt Mary quips.

"Don't forget us," Stella calls to Emma. "We have to drive to the city." Stella and Marco own a small but well-known restaurant in Manhattan and bring Emma frozen lasagna every year.

"Don't worry," Theo Sr. tells them, "there's plenty of room."

Then Emma giggles, light-headed from drinking glass after glass of rum. With eight bedrooms and a full basement with an au pair suite, she is confident there will be plenty of blankets and space for family members and friends who came from farther away. Most of their friends live close by, and Stella and Marco always have a standing invitation to stay for whatever the reason.

The noise level in the room has again become almost intolerable. *What a party!* Theo Sr. thinks, his sense of hearing numbed by the effects of the rum. In appreciation of his wife's efforts, he blows her a kiss across the room. Jennifer, who is watching her parents, winks at her dad in approval. Emma is flattered by her husband's display of affection and beams flirtatiously in return.

Emma smiles as the gifts are passed out among her guests. "Thank you!" a voice calls out. "A Coach wallet!"

"Look," another voice blares, "a Gucci key ring!"

"Ow!" one of the children shouts as he jumps up.

"Ow!" says another.

"Owww?" Aunt Mary asks. "Which designer is that, my dear child?"

"No, you don't understand. Something bit me and ran down my leg," the child complains.

"In all likelihood, it's the wood floor seam you felt," Emma guesses, "Come see what Auntie Emma bought for you, honey!"

"No, I saw something moving."

"Me too," Andy says. "And I felt it!"

"It's prob'ly jus' your imagination," Emma tells him, now slurring her words. "Where…are…my…glasses?" Emma walks toward the tree, bracing against Theo Sr. to steady her balance. Everyone is so preoccupied with opening their gifts that little attention is paid to the children.

"Thank you!" shouts Uncle Bob. "You outdid yourself this year, giving me a gift certificate for a massage and two tickets to *Jersey Boys*." *Jersey Boys?* he thinks. *I detest Jersey.*

Bernadette, Emma's partner in her previous decorating business, enters the room, regal as always with her long neck and svelte figure, holding her cocktail in one hand and a mushroom *hors d'oeuvre* in the other. As she gazes at the magnificent tree, oblivious to anything besides the glittery ornaments, she takes a bite of the mushroom pastry. It crunches, which wasn't what she expected. She eyes the appetizer and notices the hind half of a large bug oozing white liquid on top of the mushroom. Gagging, she spits out the mouthful of cockroach, retches the contents of her stomach onto the exquisite rug, and lets out a long, piercing scream!

A pause, then a feeling of panic spreads throughout the room. Children drop their presents to the floor. "What is it? What?" the adults want to know. The children brush frantically at their clothes as if they were on fire and start running off in all directions—bugs are crawling on them!

The decibel level rises again. The doorbell rings. The dogs bark wildly.

"Murphy, be quiet!" Emma orders. "Theo, where are you? What is going on?"

"Look, look!" Uncle Rodney shouts to Aunt Mary.

Stella, distracted by the commotion, slips on an area rug, slides with her legs out in front of her, and falls squarely on her bottom with an audible "thud." Startled by Stella's fall, Pookie bites her ankle. Aunt Tilly picks up her poodle, drops her on a chair, runs off without her shoes on or with any idea of where she is going, and steps on a couple of roaches as she makes her way out the front door into the cold.

"Oh, Andy, you were right!" screams Aunt Mary. There are bugs!"

Stella, a corpulent woman, hoists herself up on the sofa. When she leans over to examine her ankle, her hair brushes against her face, and out of the corner of her eye she glimpses a roach fighting its way out of her gnarled tangle. Screaming, she stands up, balancing her considerable weight on her one good leg as she attempts to whack the insect off her head. The seams of her dress rip apart all the way from her torso to below her knees, exposing the flesh of her waist cascading over her pantyhose like the top of an oversized muffin.

Theo Jr. rushes over to Stella. He swats at her head to get rid of the roach, but because she is writhing, he smacks her pudgy white skin instead. The scene is dramatic, reminiscent of a murder occurring onstage in an opera.

When the front bell rings, the door is already open a crack—and there stand the Guldsteins, just in time for the real party to get underway!

Chapter Nine

SURPRISE UNDER THE CHRISTMAS TREE

Theo Sr. tries to make his way through the melée of family and friends scrambling to stand up. The tree has been knocked over and is leaning haphazardly against the wall. The children are out of control—the girls are crying, and the boys are yelling as they play a game, stepping on as many bugs as they can to see who crushes the most.

Aunt Tilly's high-pitched shrieks pierce through the entire room as she pronounces the dreaded word—bugs! "Bugs! There are so many bugs! Bugs! Do you hear me? Bugs! Andy was right! They are huge!" She flings her arms wildly about and then wrings her hands frantically when she sees one of them slowly making its way up her precious Pookie's spine in the direction of her neck. The bug hesitates, and Aunt Tilly freezes in place, barely breathing, her eyes widened, frightened beyond words.

Theo Jr. grabs one of the cloth napkins and crushes the beetle, leaving Pookie's fur plastered with white ooze from the dead carcass. Aunt Tilly swoons for a moment, and then pushes Pookie off her lap onto the rug. Everyone in the entire house is panicked.

"Bugs?" Emma shouts. "Not in my house!"

"Bugs!" yell the guests, as if they were screaming "Fire!" at the sound of an alarm. "Bugs, bugs, bugs!" they call out as they all stand up, some on the furniture, trying to balance their plates of food in the air but letting go from fear as they squeamishly look down.

Food and pieces of Emma's fine china litter the rug and floor. She tries to fix the tree, but its heavy trunk and branches are flat against the wall and she needs help. She doesn't see that some of her Swarovski bulbs have been shattered. She hasn't seen any bugs crawling on the floor. The room is a blur, first of all, because she isn't wearing her glasses, and secondly because she is verging on being "extremely sloshed" or totally drunk.

"There are crumbs on the floor, and that is all!" Emma maintains. "That's what's making those crunching sounds. Theodore, get my glasses, please!"

Little Derek pulls on Emma's skirt, looks up and says, "There are bugs, Auntie Emma! I saw them moving, and they're ginormous!" He holds his small hands up to show her how big they are.

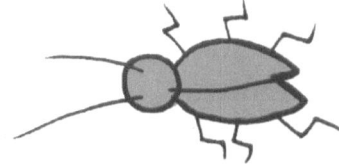

"Bring me a broom, now!" Theo Sr. orders Emma.

"Why do we need a broom?" she wonders. "This is a party!"

In the same breath Theo Sr. introduces the Guldsteins, who are standing inside the foyer, trying to make sense of the chaotic scene. "And these are the Guldsteins, dear, our new neighbors from next door, remember?" he says cordially, hoping the introduction will distract his wife from the increasing pandemonium.

Gerry and Stephanie cannot believe these are the same neighbors. "Please bring the broom to me, and then I'm sure the Guldsteins would like to take a tour of our house, dear, beginning with the upstairs," Theo Sr. continues. "You know your way, don't you, dear?"

What he fears most is Emma actually seeing the creeping black insects, which are so enormous they would unsettle anyone. He is sure they will give her a case of hives.

Theo Jr. descends the stairway after finding his mother's glasses in her bedroom, but balks at giving them to her and conceals them in his pocket. He joins his mother, attempting to calm her, while another group of bugs appears, running in various directions. The dark wood floors are laden with them, so it is hard to discern the floor from the beetles. Loud, shrill screams fill the entire first floor, drowning out the background music.

Despite her light-headedness, Emma stands in the spacious foyer, trying to remain a gracious hostess to the new neighbors. Stephanie is in awe of the house, and, though she wants to tell Emma how beautiful her house is, she can't get out the words— a highly unusual occurrence for her.

Theo Sr. notices the red hives on Emma's face. He insists the bugs came from the flowers, but Emma refuses to hear him. She is so disturbed by the idea of having bugs in her home it is nearly impossible for her to speak. Her hair is out of place, and she appears frazzled.

Emma manages to pull herself together for the Guldsteins' sake and says to them, "So glad you came. Let's go upstairs, and I'll show you the rest of the house while everyone else is dancing. You should see the bedrooms and the bathrooms. We redecorated this year."

"Dancing?" Stephanie asks while giving Gerry a glance.

"Oh, it's a party, you know," Emma says. "They're doing one of those new dances. The kids started, and then everyone else joined in."

Now Emma's anxiety shows in the way she joins her sentences together into one elongated phrase, speaking so rapidly the Guldsteins have difficulty following her. Bewildered, she stands there with her neighbors, whose attention is focused on the bedlam in the house and the hives on her face.

Stephanie edges closer to Emma and whispers in her ear, "Are you allergic to anything?"

"Why do you ask?" Emma replies, utterly confused about the reason anyone would want to know, but she doesn't pursue it further. "Shall we go upstairs?"

Gerry fears the scene is too far gone for the Wilkersens to recover, and Stephanie is sure they didn't intend the party to go this way. Still, it wasn't totally clear to everyone what was happening and how it happened.

Uncle Bob is taking it all in, watching his family fall to pieces, all the while flashing pictures and loving it. "Go up, Em. Take your guests on a grand tour for Christmas," he laughs.

He is hardly unnerved by the bugs, nor do mice or rats alarm him. He lives in the city and isn't afraid of these familiar critters. "You've got bugs, all right," he calmly tells Theo Sr., "and you have 'em bad! Look around, Theo, you're in denial."

"What do you mean, I've got 'em bad? They are bugs from the flowers Emma ordered for the party."

"Oh no, they're not," Uncle Bob gloats, certain he is right. "Bugs from flowers aren't attracted to cake."

"My dear wife ordered far too many flowers from the florist," Theo Sr. argues. "They are beetles!"

"No, no, no, they're not!" Uncle Bob replies.

"There must be a nest or some other reasonable

explanation," Theo Sr. rationalizes.

"No, my dear brother-in-law, no explanation is necessary," states Bob. "They are not beetles! They are cockroaches, and you are infested with them!"

Hearing that, a female guest emits a bloodcurdling scream. "Either you've had them for a while, or one of your guests brought them as a surprise Christmas gift!"

Theo Sr.'s knees buckle as he sits down on a chair cushion spattered with food. Family members, who have eavesdropped on his conversation with Uncle Bob, are also convinced the bugs are cockroaches.

"You've outdone yourself with the drinks this year," Uncle Bob quips. "They are outstanding—the bomb!"

Another wave of hysteria arises. Emma's great aunt faints to the floor, and her wig falls off, landing exactly where Murphy and Pookie are eating spilled vegetables off the rug. Murphy latches onto the impeccably coiffed hair while Pookie pulls at the other end in a tug-of-war. Both dogs hold on tight until the wig rips in two. Murphy reigns victorious, shaking his head from side to side with the larger piece of wig in his mouth.

Jennifer chokes, stifling her laughter at the sight of her bald-headed aunt. Unable to contain herself, she runs to the kitchen, followed by Uncle Bob, who tells her to bring a cloth saturated with ammonia to rouse her aunt.

The guests scatter into other rooms, upstairs or

downstairs, and even out into the blizzard, thinking they can escape from the vile creatures. Barefoot, the women race into the front yard, shivering so violently in the snow they look like they are doing a dance that is a cross between James Brown and Axl Rose. One woman is so hysterical she runs out the door into the freezing cold, stumbling into a snowbank headfirst. Then, without her coat, she drives away in the family car, leaving her husband and children behind, their mouths agape. Dumbfounded, they peer out the door, watching her take off.

A frazzled couple on their way out offers them a ride home. After locating their coats beneath the debris, they leave together. "There's a cockroach climbing up my sleeve inside my jacket!" a child cries out, and they all undo their coats, letting them slip off their shoulders into the drifting snow.

At the rear of the Wilkersens' home, two young couples race to the pool area to flee the roaches. Without hesitation they run across the canvas that covers the water. They overlook the other end, where the canvas is rolled back. Sinking in a few inches, they emerge on the other side, wet up to their knees, staring down at what happened to their beautiful party clothes. "Oh, my dress, my shoes!" the women moan. "The water is freezing cold!"

Sitting in a darkened corner near the shallow end of the pool is Aunt Bell, dressed almost entirely in leopard print, smoking a cigarette in her mother-of-pearl cigarette holder, knowing full well no smoking is allowed in the house. With her is Jack, her only son. Thinking she is special, surely better than the other guests, she remains separate from the party, as does snobby, clumsy Jack, who also has an unrealistically high opinion of himself.

Despite her supercilious airs, she sees the couples are in need of help. She forces Jack to bring back towels from one of the guest bathrooms, even though he couldn't care less about helping anyone but himself. Then, as silently as she arrived, she departs, conducting herself as if nothing out of the ordinary was happening, maintaining the cool exterior of someone who would never admit her fear. Behind her is Jack, tripping over himself, not able to get away fast enough from the tumultuous scene playing out in front of his eyes.

The dogs are barking wildly. Emma feels weak and sits down on the sofa with Jennifer, who puts the bottle of ammonia down on the floor, holds her mother's hand and fans her, ready with the rag to revive her if she faints. Jennifer's eyes are drawn to the hives that mark Emma's face, neck, and chest with raised red blotches.

Emma gazes blankly in front of her. Her skin feels itchy, and her face is hot to the touch. "Do I have bumps?" she asks.

"No, Mom. You are just fine," Jennifer replies, not wanting to add to her mother's distress. "Relax."

"How could this happen to me?" Emma wonders in a shrill crescendo.

Even the Guldsteins are trying to calm her down.

Both of them see the hordes of cockroaches and understand the reason for the madness, but Emma still doesn't fully grasp the extent of the situation. Gerry has always assumed that cockroaches live only in the city, and takes Jennifer aside to ask her if she has ever seen cockroaches in their neighborhood.

"We have never had those, ever!" she replies defensively. "Maybe a field mouse once or twice, and Mom always leaves the house until it is caught. Cockroaches? Never!"

"I'm sorry. I didn't mean to offend you," Gerry says. "We're new to the neighborhood."

"That's okay—the cockroaches are new to us."

Uncle Bob suggests to Theo Sr. that they try killing some of the roaches, but Emma insists on calling an exterminator if there are bugs, as everyone says there are. She doesn't want her feet to touch the floor, particularly because she doesn't have her glasses on.

"They are water bugs that have come inside because of the snow—I'm sure of that... Theo, Theo! Call now! My party is ruined! Bob, shut up, you're scaring everyone—there are no roaches. It's impossible! They wouldn't dare come in here!"

"That's what you think, my dear sister. And no exterminator is going to come out on Christmas Day in the middle of a blizzard to kill roaches," Uncle Bob wryly observes. "And they *are* roaches! Find your specs, my dear sister, and you'll see. Why don't you call the fire department or the police? Maybe they can get rid of your water bugs." He laughs.

The dogs yap as they slide across the slippery floor, hunting the roaches, sniffing them out of their hiding places. Murphy discovers the swatch of hair from Emma's aunt's wig, shakes it vigorously, and lets it go. It lands in the fireplace.

Within seconds the living room reeks of burnt wig, and smoke fills the room that once looked like a page out of House Beautiful. Everyone is coughing, and speaking is virtually impossible because of the noise. Some male guests attempt to crush the roaches with Emma's magazines and books, but, like Theo Sr., aren't quick enough most of the time. When they aim accurately, the magazine strikes with such force that all that is left of the roach is a flattened carcass. Under the influence of Theo Sr.'s rum, they miss far more often than they hit. Some are throwing drinks into the fireplace to extinguish the flames of the smoldering wig, but each glass of rum enflames the fire more and it rages out of control.

With a dramatic sigh Emma repeats over and over that she is faint. This has become tiresome to Jennifer, who thinks her mother is crying wolf. The women are tossing linen dinner napkins over the floor to cover the roaches and crush them with their shoe soles. Another regiment of roaches has found the buffet table and scurries across the white tablecloth, boldly attacking the leftover food. The children are excited now, running up and down the stairway with flushed cheeks, collecting cockroaches in Emma's china bowls and comparing numbers to see who has caught the most.

"How dare those things come into my home!" Emma declares, offended by the loathsome insects.

Theo Jr. has already begun to throw the contaminated food away in the kitchen barrel. Murphy begs for scraps with the pink poodle glued to his side, whining for some of her own. Jennifer holds her mother by the waist and guides her up to the first stair landing, telling her to stay there. "Mom, we'll take care of it," she says. "The Guldsteins are waiting for you."

The Guldsteins remain downstairs at the foot of the wide staircase, perplexed about why the Wilkersens' house suddenly has roaches—not just a few, but a breeding ground. It reminds them of their old apartment the first time they saw the roaches marching out of a hole in the kitchen wall all over the counters and floors when a new tenant moved in. Their minds are racing—these critters are the same size as the ones in the old apartment.

Guilt-prone Stephanie believes she and Gerry are somehow to blame for the appearance of the cockroaches. "Gerr, I feel ill," she says.

"Steph—please don't even go there. We'd better leave."

"It can't be, can it?" she whispers. "We don't have any roaches at our new house, do we, honey? Are you keeping something from me?"

"No, dear, there are no secrets. I'm not certain what is happening here, but let's get the hell out, fast!" Gerry finds their coats, and they head in the direction of the front door.

"Stay!" Emma calls out to them. "Stay for dessert. I'm feeling much better, and I'll take you on a tour. I wouldn't want you to leave because you're frightened! They are beetles or water bugs, I assure you!"

"We came to say only a quick hello," Gerry said. "We didn't realize my mother cooked for us, and she will be insulted if we don't eat her food. You know how mothers are... We told her not to bother, but she did anyway. She's highly sensitive to rejection—a real Jewish mother."

"The baby isn't feeling well," Stephanie adds as an excuse, biting her tongue. "She's cutting a new tooth."

"We'll come again soon," Gerry says. "It looks like a great party!"

The Guldsteins step closer to the front door, open it, and can't run off fast enough.

Emma couldn't be more upset than she was at that moment. *What will our other neighbors think?* she worries, as she stomps her foot down on the floor like a child demanding candy. As her foot strikes the carpet, she unknowingly crushes a half-dead cockroach, and its sticky guts adhere to the bottom of her shoe. "Theo, where are you?" she shouts as she collides into a wall.

The Guldsteins wade hurriedly through the high snowdrifts of the Wilkersens' front lawn toward home. Stephanie comments on how refreshing the snow feels as it falls on her face. Gerry agrees.

They quickly enter their house and stare through the curtains at the madness outside their neighbors' elegant home. They were so hungry before they arrived there, but now they have lost their appetites.

Stephanie notices they both forgot to remove their boots at the entrance and had made the rugs wet. "A wet rug is better than a sea of cockroaches," she says.

"Stephanie, did we bring the roaches with us?" Gerry inquires. "Or perhaps it was the caterers?"

"Yes, it must have been the caterers," she replies. "We couldn't have brought that many." She stands motionless as a mannequin as he removes her coat. "At least I *hope* it was the caterers. The movers and exterminators told us to get rid of the boxes right away, and we did...but, oh no!"

In sudden shock, Stephanie covers her face with the palms of her hands. "The boxes!" she cries out. "It must have been the boxes in the back yard! We put them against the fence, and the doors were wide open while the caterers were carrying in the food."

She is getting more anxious by the moment. "We have to get rid of those boxes! But how? They may see us hauling them away."

She absentmindedly takes Roger's dry towel from its hook and wipes the floor in the foyer. Nana hears them at the front door and asks, "Why is the door open? The draft is like polar winds. You both will catch your deaths of cold! What kind of party is it with everyone running and jumping, hitting the floor with dishrags?"

"Ma, why are you spying on them?" Gerry snaps.

"And women out in the snow without coats!" Nana continues. "Why are some people sitting in their cars without going anywhere? Is it some kind of game? And why didn't you remove your boots? You tramped snow into the house! That certainly is out of character. What did you do, smoke a crazy cigarette over there?"

"Ma, please stop! We didn't smoke anything," Gerry insists, promising her he will explain later. "C'mon, honey, we have to think of a plan," he tells Stephanie.

"Plan? What plan? So it is a game," Nana surmises.

Stephanie shakes her head, discouraged. "No, Ma, it's not a game."

"Maybe you want to talk about it?" presses Nana.

Stephanie doesn't feel like speaking, but tells her mother-in-law they were so cold they had forgotten about taking off their boots, and left the door wide open by mistake.

"You know, Ma," Gerry says, "it would be better if you minded your own you-know-what. If you must know, Stephanie is upset because she wasn't as dressed up as the other women." He bites his tongue as he tells that lie.

Consumed by the thought that she has caused their neighbors' plight, Stephanie thinks how furious she would be in their position had they brought cockroaches into her home, especially on a holiday when they were entertaining with a house full of family and guests. She wonders if she has done the right thing by leaving rather than staying to help kill the roaches she detests so much.

Perhaps we are at fault, she ponders.

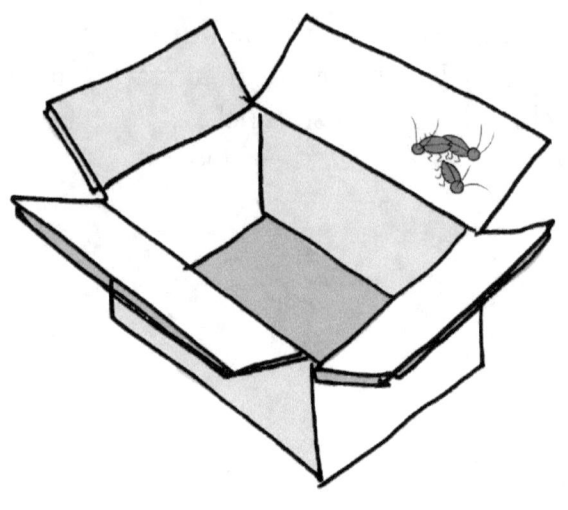

Chapter Ten

GETTING RID OF THE EVIDENCE

Gerry's mother and father are at a loss trying to account for the neighbors' behavior. Both are beginning to doubt the wisdom of their son's move.

"They must be the kind of people who drink too much," Nana says. "What do you think?"

"No, Ma, they are decent people having a good time. They know the difference between right and wrong."

Gerry and Stephanie need a plan to remove the pile of boxes from the Wilkersens' back yard without being seen. They could see small groups of people loitering in the atrium, a glass structure near the pool with full-length windows. Though the boxes are covered with snow, a spotlight shines directly on that part of the fence. If by chance anyone looks out the back windows, they would see Gerry and Stephanie moving the boxes, attracting attention to themselves as the culprits.

Gerry recalls Theo Sr. mentioning having used the same caterers for the past ten years without any concerns at all, especially about cleanliness.

"Oh no, then it was us!" she groans.

"Yes, I'm afraid it was," Gerry admits.

They resign themselves to confessing their responsibility to the Wilkersens at some point, but not just yet. "Later on, when the exterminators eventually arrive, they may connect the cardboard boxes in the yard with the roaches," Stephanie points out. "Then our relationship with the Wilkersens will be less than cordial."

Worried, they watch as the cars parked on their neighbors' yard and driveway leave in the blizzard. Yet some cars remain, despite the pandemonium and the weather, both of which are worsening by the moment. Stephanie assumes the guests who left were more intimidated by the cockroaches than by the treacherous snow.

"When would be the right time to acknowledge that it was us?" Gerry asks his wife. "When?" Confused and upset, she offers no response.

He sits down beside Roger, who looks up at him with sad brown eyes. "Hey, Rog, what do you think?" Roger barks once, rolls over and plays dead. "You see, honey? Even Roger knows we're dead dogs."

Stephanie laughs.

"Do we have any bones in the refrigerator, Steph? I promised Roger bones or leftovers from the party. Since we didn't take any scraps, he'll have to eat my mom's brisket. Perhaps we should have taken Roger so he could've eaten all the food he wanted."

"Nah, the roaches would have gotten stuck in his fur," she says.

"Yeah, but he could have been a companion to Murphy and helped him out with the cockroaches."

"Nah, Roger would have blown our cover by killing the roaches and dropping them at my feet, the same as he used to do in the apartment."

Gerry can't stop laughing at the thought of Murphy skidding across the Wilkersens' floor, nipping at the huge, scurrying bugs. His laughter is infectious. Stephanie can't stop giggling about the burning wig. She laughs until she no longer can, then becomes still, panic beginning to set in.

"Stop laughing, honey," she says to her husband. We must have roaches, too! Where's my flashlight, Gerr? They are hiding, waiting to come out! Let's look...please, I know they're here! I know it! We'll have to throw everything away!"

"Oh no, I can't believe this! Hey, hey, stop, Steph. They're not here! They're over there!"

"Very funny!"

"Steph, we would have seen them by now." Gerry tries to appease her, speaking slowly and precisely. "Calm yourself. We have no bugs. Look around, don't you remember the exterminator said to throw out all the boxes immediately and we wouldn't have problems?"

"Yes. We took the cartons out as fast as was humanly possible. The roaches obviously stayed inside the cardboard. That's where they hid." Her voice strains. "They could be hiding behind our walls—they multiply so quickly."

"We'll get an exterminator, okay, honey? I'll call tomorrow."

"The roaches must have gone to the closest house, the one that smelled of food. And they might be hiding in our TVs, waiting to come out tonight or when we least expect it."

"No," Gerry insists. "They're not in the TVs."

"We will be watching the news, and they'll walk across the TV screen. I just know it! What will happen when we call an exterminator? The Wilkersens will think it was us."

"No. They'll think we're being cautious. Steph, you're being paranoid."

"The exterminator didn't tell us they would go somewhere else or that they could withstand the freezing temperature trooping over to the neighbors' house. When they escaped, some of them might have gone to others' houses. I just know it!"

"No hon, the other neighbors have gone away for the holiday. Stop freaking out!"

"Let's look, we have to!" Stephanie pleads, as she begins looking in and under everything in sight.

"Let's just remain calm," Gerry reiterates. "My

mom and dad will hear you."

Nana enters the room. She couldn't stay away, so attracted by Stephanie's high-pitched voice.

"So what is this mysterious subject you cannot discuss in front of me?" she inquires. "And Stephanie, what are you doing, and why are you so nervous, my dear daughter-in-law?"

"Oh, Mom, I didn't hear you come in!" says Gerry, surprised by his mother's sudden appearance.

"You both look like you've just robbed a bank. What happened next door?"

"Mom, we can't talk right now," Gerry says, looking directly into his mother's eyes as he fabricates his excuse. "We have to clean."

"Clean?" Nana asks. "I just cleaned. You need stronger glasses!"

"I'm sorry, Ma. I mean rearrange the furniture. We want to move it around differently."

"Again? Are you both on drugs?"

"No, Ma, don't be crazy. I want to change the furniture around. We're still adjusting to the house."

"Again you want to change it? *Oy vey!* You've both been peculiar since you moved in here, two *meshugenas!*" she admonishes them, wagging her finger in Gerry's direction.

His dad enters. "Yes, son," he says, "both of you have been acting oddly since you moved. Maybe the stress of moving has been too much for you."

Stephanie urges her in-laws to go upstairs, nudging them toward the staircase.

"Both of you came back nuts since going to the

party next door," Nana persists. "What were they doing over there? Did you smoke marijuana?"

Gerry chokes with laughter as he watches his mother make the motions of sucking on a joint. Grandpa's eye twinkles and he chuckles along with his son.

"All they did was drink, maybe more than usual because of the holiday, but there weren't any drugs, Ma. Where did you get the idea they were doing drugs, anyway?"

"I've seen the way addicts crawl on the floor looking for drugs on TV, you know, all the cop and detective shows. But all right, all right, I'm going. I can tell when I'm not wanted."

Oh no, there she goes with her guilt shtick again, Gerry thinks, and then tells her worriedly, "Ma, I have more pressing issues to attend to."

Gerry is starting to get worried, *Maybe when Theo Sr. finally discovers the roaches came from here, he'll want to get revenge. He might bring cockroaches to our house and let them loose here. Even worse, he could give us mice or rats!* Tense, he holds his head between his hands.

As Nana and Grandpa go up the stairs, Stephanie and Gerry turn off the downstairs lights, grab another flashlight, and sit down by a living-room window, resting their elbows on the sill and cupping their chins in their hands as they eye the continuing turmoil at the Wilkersens' house.

"Those poor people. We did this, honey," Stephanie says remorsefully.

"Yes, I believe we did, and Mom was right—they

do look like addicts scrounging the floor for drugs. With all their lights on, we have a perfect view."

However, the snow is now so heavy no spaces are visible between the falling flakes—just one big white sheet.

"I feel so badly, Stephanie," Gerry admits.
Roger comes over and jumps into his master's lap. He whines, as if he senses their discomfort. He lies down on the floor and rolls over with his legs in the air, doing his dead-dog routine. Gerry and Stephanie laugh. Thanks to Roger, they forget their troubles, if only for a few minutes.

Chapter Eleven

CHRISTMAS WITH THE COCKROACHES

Poor Emma is a total washed-out mess. She hasn't looked in a mirror since late morning, when she went up to her room to try on more bracelets— six weren't enough. She had no time to look for others, and no one dared tell her that her face is blotched. Had Emma looked at her reflection, she wouldn't have been able to see it anyway.

Without her contacts (which she misplaced on Christmas Eve) or her glasses, Emma is legally blind. Neither Theo Sr. nor Theo Jr. was in a hurry to give Emma her spare glasses. Theo Jr. avoids his mother, so she won't ask him for her glasses, which are still hidden in his pants pocket. He is certain she would faint if she could see clearly.

Uncle Bob finds the situation hilarious, though

he is concerned about how his sister's mental state will be by the end of the evening. As he roars with laughter, he holds onto his small potbelly. He cannot keep himself from laughing.

Emma is a wreck. She can sense what is happening and isn't the least bit amused. Her elegant designer dress is wrinkled, and soiled by spilled food. A wide chocolate mark stains the front. Her hands are filthy, covered in the supper they had just consumed. The custom-made floors are slathered with food debris and puddles of drinks knocked over in the brouhaha.

Emma's strident voice rises above the others as she calls out, "Theo, Theo, where are you?"

Cockroaches, alive and dead, are strewn about. The guests who have stayed cannot escape the chaos, but because of the amount of rum they are drinking they don't care.

Aunt Mary is eating food from the buffet table, food Theo Jr. is about to throw away. Jennifer suspects she must have eaten a bug or two. Some family members are leaving the house to sit in their cars for a moment of peace. Others have left, outraged, saying, "Well, I never…"

Aunt Mary is now striding from room to room, clutching her hair as if she wants to pull it out, stopping every so often to sample a *hors d'oeuvre*.

Emma's once beautiful home now imparts the impression of an asylum for the severely mentally ill—on a really bad day.

Out of the corner of his eye, Uncle Bob catches

Emma swallowing a tiny Valium she keeps in the kitchen silverware drawer for emergencies.

Murphy and Pookie are having the time of their lives, tasting every kind of food on the floor, lapping up the rum-laced eggnog, eating the carcasses of a few crushed cockroaches. The dogs are becoming friends after years of rivalry.

"Oh my poor Pookie!" wails Aunt Tilly. "Come to Mommy. You'll have to see a vet!"

Pookie ignores her. She no longer barks, but now rests quietly next to Murphy, feeling slightly drunk. She is so content she lies across Murphy's front legs.

"Oh, my poor, poor baby," Aunt Tilly moans. "Come sit on Mommy's lap. You're not of sound mind."

Theo Jr. is relieved that "Pinky Poo" is behaving like a real dog instead of being Aunt Tilly's toy. His uncle is in stitches watching her fall apart. Theo Jr. glances at Jennifer, placing two fingers down his throat to show how he feels about his aunt.

The bet is on. Uncle Bob makes a wager with Theo Sr. and Emma that no exterminator will come out on Christmas day in a snowstorm. After a long series of telephone calls and more rum, Emma has almost resigned herself to living with the roaches until an exterminator agrees to come. She considers going to a hotel, but Theo Sr. talks her out of that.

"We will deal with this!" he says firmly, "This is not a mouse we are talking about, Emma. We are going to take care of this cockroach problem head-on, all of us, including you, Emma. No more attitude. No more of a lot of things after this Christmas!"

"And what exactly does that mean?" Emma inquires.

"You'll see, Emma. You'll see!"

Theo Jr. cheers on his father's newfound resolve, "Yeah, you go, Dad!"

"Just pretend you are in a dream," Theo Sr. tells Emma. Intoxicated and almost asleep, she finds his suggestion plausible. Her vision is hazy at best, and she confuses people's names, if she remembers them at all.

Uncle Bob tells her that this Christmas is the first real celebration he has enjoyed with the family since they were kids. Emma doesn't yet understand what he means and is peeved by his remark.

"What is that supposed to mean?" she slurs. "You don't like my parties? All these years and you never told me?"

"Oh yes, I've tried, my dear sister."

She drinks even more, and has had quite enough when Theo Sr. takes the glass from her hand.

"Hey, hey, give me my drink!"

"No, Emma, I'm telling you *no*."

She grabs the phone and calls 911. Theo Sr. tries to stop her to avoid the embarrassment of making an emergency call to the police about bugs—and not just any kind of bug, but cockroaches. The cop on the other end, knowing there aren't any cockroaches in her neighborhood and hearing her slurred speech from intoxication, wishes Mrs. Wilkersen happy holidays and thanks her for the generous donation she made to their fund this year and in past years.

"Have a great Christmas with the cockroaches!" he calls out amid the laughter in the background. Cautioning her not to drive, he politely hangs up.

"They think I'm drunk," she says.

"Well, you are dear," Theo Sr. reminds her.

"I am sober," she insists. "How dare they! They wished me a Merry Christmas with the cockroaches. Oh, excuse me. I did not see you there."

"See whom?" Theo Sr. asks.

"Never mind," she says. "Would you get me another drink, Theo, please?"

"Emma, you've had enough, I'm telling you. That's it—I'm putting my foot down!"

"You go, Dad!" Jennifer cheers, putting her hands above her head. Theo Jr. joins his sister's plaudits for their father, clapping his hands.

"I think it might be time to put on your glasses so you won't mistake the lamp for a person," Uncle Bob tells Emma. "Why don't you rest upstairs?"

"I still don't have my glasses, and I don't want to go up!" she protests.

"I'll take care of all this," Theo Sr. interjects.

"I refuse to lie in a roach-infested bed!" she declares. "And I do not need my glasses. I can see perfectly well. Everything is fine. It's just that they're dancing one of those new dances. The extra staff left, so now there's no one to clean up. It's not bugs, it's the music!"

"Okay, dear, whatever you say." He takes a dead cockroach, holds it inside a napkin and shows it up close to his wife. "Emma, my dear, do you see this?"

"Oh, is it a piece of Belgian chocolate?" she slurs.

"No, dear, it's not."

"Theo, I will not go anywhere until the exterminators are here! I will stay up the entire night if I have to!"

Sure that it will be a matter of time until his wife passes out and falls asleep, Theo Sr. says, "Come, Emma, sit on the chair."

"No, I want to sit on the couch."

"No chair! No couch! No!" Jennifer suddenly shouts as she goes over to check them for bugs, but it is too late—Emma is already sprawled on the down sofa, her eyes opening and closing, her head resting on her fabulous white pillows that are now smeared with the guts of crushed roaches. Both Uncle Bob and Theo Sr. bet she will be asleep in a few minutes—and they win!

Jennifer, Aunt Mary, and Uncle Bob clean off the couch stains as best they can while Emma snores contentedly. Then, just as they think she is out cold, the doorbell chimes.

Emma leaps up from the sofa. "There they are!"

"No, Mom, it's not them. Sit down, please!"

"See, Theo dear, I told you they would come!"

Again, Jennifer tells her mother to sit, that her friends are at the door, not the exterminators. "Dad, help me out here! I called them and left our address."

"It's them!" Emma exclaims.

"It's *not* them," Jennifer insists as she tenses her jaw and grinds her teeth. "It's after six. You were the one who told me to have my friends come now, Mom. Sit down. Let me handle this, please. I don't want them to see you or our house."

"Our house is 'bee-yoo-ti-ful,' Emma slurs. "And as for me, I'm bee-yoo-ti-ful too."

Though everyone makes their best effort to clean up, roaches are still crawling on the floor. Emma pushes Jennifer aside and answers the bell, looking disheveled and worn, her face swollen with red blotches and bumps, her thinking muddled, and her sight blurred. She leans against the door and holds it open for Jennifer's friends. At first she thinks the exterminators have arrived because of the boxes they are holding, but then she sees they are gifts.

"Let them in, Emma dear!" yells Theo Sr.

"Come on in, girls," Emma says, running her words together and looking behind the girls to make sure the exterminators aren't there.

"Oooh," they say as they enter the hallway, which is littered with spilled drinks and dishrags. "What happened here? Are you okay, Mrs. W.?"

"I'm just ducky," Emma replies.

Jennifer steps in front of her mother, almost pushing her aside. "Dad!" she yells, "Please take Mom—she's tired from cooking all day!"

She advises her friends to go directly up to her room. "Don't look around," she tells them. "I'll explain later."

"Oooh, your mom is wasted," one of them says. "And she cooks now? Does she take lessons?"

"No, not really. She's tired from being up all day,

you know, taking the food from the refrigerator to the table."

The family disperses throughout the once-perfect house, still hitting the bugs on the floor with anything within reach while consuming Theo Sr.'s rum. Jennifer hurries her friends up the stairs, but they turn their heads to gawk at the scene below, using their cell phone camera phones to capture it.

"When did your mom start cooking on Christmas?" another friend asks. All of them giggle. Jennifer, in no laughing mood, half smiles with a look of extreme discomfort.

Strangely, in what seemed like only a moment, the panic that engulfed the room earlier has turned into laughter. Uncle Bob, joyous as ever, tells a few jokes, some about cockroaches. The air feels lighter, and all are enjoying themselves, as if suddenly aware of real life. Aunt Mary has gone to refill her empty glass. The guests' alarm has given way to acceptance of the bizarre situation. They are now laid back, almost serene.

The two Theos pride themselves on killing the largest number of cockroaches, and as they sweep up, they swear never to forget this Christmas.

Theo Jr. comments, "Yeah, Dad, gotta tell you that this was the best Christmas, the most exciting Christmas ever." He giggles uncontrollably, "I especially enjoyed seeing all my aunts with their eyelashes unglued."

Emma, however, is still ranting, repeating over and over again that she wants to move out of the house tonight, right now, and buy a new one.

Theo Sr. and others in the family try to reassure her that it is just one night and the cockroaches will be gone. "And, Emma," he says, "we're not moving." He gently pulls her close and kisses her like old times. "After this Christmas, our traditions will be changing!"

Aunt Tilly can't bear to pick up Pookie, who is damp with eggnog and matted with food in her fur. Her pink toenails are scuffed from slipping across the floor. Less than perfect now, she is less than haughty.

Aunt Tilly expresses regret to Emma that she won't be visiting ever again.

Her husband, however, has never been happier. "I'll be back, with or without Tilly and the dog," he says joyfully. "This is the best party I've ever been to." He assures Theo Sr. that he will be back to visit any time they extend an invitation, not just for Christmas.

Theo Jr. stands by his Uncle Bob, smiling the widest of grins at him.

Aunt Tilly, feeling left out, launches into one of her fits. Tears roll down her cheeks, destroying her perfectly made-up face, as she stomps her feet and rants to herself. Pookie senses her mistress's distress and comes to her side.

Uncle Bob, still in high spirits, continues to drink, laugh, and photograph Aunt Tilly and the entire house and family. He can't wait to share those shots with his friends, especially those of Aunt Tilly and

Aunt Mary. They are priceless, the icing on the cake, jauntily chronicling the slapstick that turned this Christmas celebration upside-down from the moment he stepped through the door. This year's holiday photos capture Uncle Bob's family and friends as they really are—flawed, like the rest of us.

One question is yet to be answered, though: where did the cockroaches come from? In fact, that has become the main topic of conversation. Theo Sr. assures Emma he will get to the bottom of the whole mess later, once the holiday has passed. He expresses his gratitude towards his family and friends for their help and understanding in this situation, and for sticking through the whole ordeal.

For this Christmas with the cockroaches taught him who his true friends are and which family he can trust without question. It was a special holiday for that reason, though Emma has yet to appreciate it.

Chapter Twelve

QUIET IN THE NIGHT

Finally, after hours of chaos, the panic about the roaches eases, and the Wilkersens and their guests quiet down, yawning and stretching. Rather than gossip, they talk about matters that mean something to them: everyday occurrences, what touches their hearts, real problems, or other subjects they rarely discussed before. Unlike other Christmas holidays at the Wilkersens, no one says a critical word about anyone else, but takes a genuine interest in others' lives.

It is late, and they are exhausted, beat by the excitement of the day. Christmas Day is giving way to night, and the snow has almost stopped, leaving over sixteen inches on the ground. Everyone comments on how beautiful it looks as they gather together in front of the window, gazing at the snow, feeling the warmth of the fireplace, hearing the sporadic crackles of dead cockroaches in the fire.

Jennifer found skewers and marshmallows in the kitchen, and they roast them by the fire as if on a camping trip, sitting on the floor like Indians smoking a peace pipe. They are not concerned about proper etiquette or dropping anything on the floor. The atmosphere is so relaxed the marshmallows seem to taste better than Emma's pricey pastries. Even she is eating marshmallows from the skewer, requesting them to be slightly browned and crispy, the way she ate them as a child.

The company is somewhat hung over from the fruity rum drinks. The Christmas Day panic has drained their energy. The house was overrun with roaches for hours, but for now they are out of sight. Theo Sr., Uncle Bob, and Uncle Arnold mop the floors as the rest of the company sits.

Though frightened at first, the children are calm now that evening has come, especially the girls. They had been entertained throughout the day by all the adults acting oddly, leaping from the furniture and snapping dishrags at the scuttling bugs. At last they went downstairs and passed out while watching videos.

Most of the adults forgot to open their presents. The beautifully wrapped boxes are untouched. But they don't really care about the presents now, only about helping to clean up.

Whoever wants food has to take it from the refrigerator and eat it right away where they stand so it won't attract roaches. Theo Sr. thinks it would be better not to set out plates, not just yet.

Theo Jr. shoveled a path to the end of the driveway and put trash bag after trash bag of spoiled food into barrels out in front of the house, not in the back shed out of fear that the creepy critters would re-enter his house and the neighbors' houses. He also threw away his mother's magazines.

"Oh, I hope these bugs don't go anywhere else," Emma says with sincere concern. "What will our new neighbors, the Guldsteins, think of us? They've just moved in. Can you imagine if a bug gets into their new home?"

"Don't worry," Theo Sr. reassures her. "They seem to be the nicest people—you only need to explain it to them. We could offer to pay for their extermination if you like, my dear."

Emma doesn't know what to answer.

On one of his trips to the sidewalk Theo Jr. remembered the Guldsteins' boxes piled up against the fence. "Hey, Dad, we ought to tell the neighbors they have to leave their boxes for the trash collectors out in front of the house. Especially with this bug problem. What if the roaches go into their boxes, Dad?"

"Yes, son, I'll tell them tomorrow."

Theo Jr. knows they have to tie the boxes first, just as he and Jennifer did last year when one of their chores was to dispose of the boxes from their new televisions. "Maybe I should tell them, Dad. What do you think?"

"I'll speak to Gerry the next time I take Murphy out in the morning. They must know about roaches after living in the city." He makes it clear he will take care of it; there isn't any rush because trash day is two days away and he will not forget to mention it. The Wilkersens don't even suspect their cockroach problem originated from their new neighbors' boxes.

Aunt Tilly calmed down after her outburst and doesn't seem to be the same person. She is now a relaxed version of herself. "You are just like your father," she tells Theo Jr.

He smiles, first of all because Aunt Tilly has come back to earth, and most of all because he admires his father. Theo Jr. dislikes his dad's weakness when it comes to his mom, spoiling her and giving in to her every whim. This year his dad seems to be more in control of what he considers important in their home. He told Emma to attend Theo Jr.'s games and give Jennifer's needs more attention instead of making their lives a fashion statement, like earlier in the day before the party started.

Emma actually listened to her husband when he suggested she sit down. It was the first time in years she took direction from him. This Christmas has been a momentous day in the lives of the Wilkersens and their friends and family.

The Guldsteins, meanwhile, are dreading going over to the Wilkersens. They decide not to go to tell them about the roaches until the morning, or perhaps the next day. Thoroughly drained from anxiety, they fall asleep on the couch with their flashlight still on after staring through the windows of the Wilkersens' house for hours.

It is after midnight. Hannah and Roger are asleep. The Guldsteins' house is peaceful. They searched every corner earlier, and they have no bugs, just worry.

Back at the Wilkersens', Jennifer's friends went home after she told them all the news about the roaches at the party. This turned out to be a mistake, because, when Jennifer went on Facebook before going to bed, she saw that one of her friends had taken pictures of the hallway, her mom, the tree in the living room knocked against the wall, and Pookie and Murphy spattered with food. She also photographed close-ups of the dining room, where food covered the floor and spilled drinks were in puddles containing a few drowned, floating cockroaches. The girl posted on her wall, "For a different kind of holiday cheer, look at my Facebook page: Christmas with the cockroaches at the Wilkersens' house." And then there was Jennifer's mom—her mom!—under the influence, no less sober than a drunk on the street.

Jennifer wants to choke her so-called friends. It spread all over Facebook, along with comments, "For a cock-a-roach Christmas, take a look at…roach *hors d'oeuvres* served at the Wilkersens' house…and holiday cheer—have your roach drink here!"

Thankfully, Emma and Theo Sr. are totally unaware of social media. However, Theo Jr.'s girlfriend phoned Jennifer to tell her she wouldn't be coming over to the house this week and to let Theo know. "Oh, I just hate bugs," she wrote. "I can't go anywhere that's not spotless. We will have to break up!" Jennifer tells Theo Jr. how immature his girlfriend is.

Now they are the laughingstock of Long Island! What will happen when Theo Sr. and Emma go out on the town? Will this ruin their lives in Long Island, or will they stand up to these rich biddies? As Uncle Bob puts it, "Bump 'em if they can't take a joke!" To counter all the tomfoolery, Jennifer and Theo Jr. put on their Facebook pages that their Christmas was the best they've had in years.

The Wilkersens leave on as many lights as possible so the bugs, they hope, will stay away. Uncle Bob is in tears from laughing so hard all night. "You think that the roaches are gone because you can't see them?" He bursts out into more chuckles.

Everyone goes to bed wherever they land, sleeping fitfully for the rest of the night. Murphy and Pookie lie down at the foot of the fireplace, side by side, without Emma or Aunt Tilly. Aunt Tilly and Uncle Arnold are holding hands as they climb the stairway to their guest bedroom, retiring together for the first time in years.

Chapter Thirteen

MYSTERY NOT SOLVED

Morning comes. All of the lights in the Wilkersen household are still on, despite the blinding sunshine that reflects off the snow and floods through their windows. Complaints of headaches and hangovers are heard. All showers and sinks are running. Aspirin tablets are passed out like jellybeans, as well as the new toothbrushes Emma had ready for emergency situations such as snowstorms and hurricanes. Theo Sr. makes Bloody Marys and mimosas for those whose hangovers are best treated with the hair of the dog that bit them.

Because their holiday meal had been disrupted, everyone is hungry. All refrigerators are full, and Uncle Bob plays chef, cooking up a breakfast feast.

Emma has never allowed him in her kitchen before, though he is an accomplished cook. The inviting smell of bacon wafts through the house. He stayed the night and was up early cleaning and contacting the exterminators, who made an appointment to come later in the afternoon. Happier than ever, he is singing out loud, wearing Emma's frilly fitted apron wrapped around his middle, accentuating his pot belly.

It is a new day and the beginning of a new way of life. The house had been nightmarish on Christmas Day, but the family that stayed isn't discussing it. They don't seem to care.

Emma is so relieved that Bob took the initiative to clean up and to help put an end to their cockroach problem. She hugs and kisses him, and thanks her brother.

"It feels like when we were kids," she says.

Emma isn't the least bit concerned about how her home appears. In fact, she wasn't upset when she finally put on her glasses. When Uncle Bob wishes Emma a Merry Christmas, to his surprise she holds on to him, hugging him back even more. A few tears well up in her swollen eyes, and Uncle Bob sheds a tear or two of his own; both of them remembering precious memories from their past, when they regularly hugged each other on Christmas Day.

Family members volunteer to clean up, wearing sweatpants borrowed from Theo Jr. and Jennifer, some still dressed in the glittery tops they wore the day before. None of the women apply make-up—not even Emma, who says she prefers to appear natural this Christmas.

"You look even more beautiful," Theo Sr. tells her.

"Do I?" she replies. "I feel fine. I feel free. Now I understand the reason you didn't want to give me my glasses!"

"Yes, dear, but it's okay now. It's even better than okay." They hugged like when they first dated. A romantic, deep hug, with them clinging to each other passionately and staying in each other's arms much longer than was their norm.

Back at the Guldsteins, Gerry and Stephanie awoke extremely early in the morning. They still felt stressed from the day before, but needed to tend to Hannah and, of course, Roger. To avoid running into Theo Sr., Gerry took Roger to the other side of the house beside the garage at 7:00 a.m.

As difficult as it had been to do, the night before they had written a long letter to the Wilkersens apologizing for bringing the cockroaches from Manhattan. They offered to pay for all of the cleaning and extermination expenses, as well as inviting them out to dinner to any place they wished to go, paying for the meal and extras. The Guldsteins had also invited the Wilkersens for New Year's Day dinner at their house, in case the party had upset their routine so much they would decide to stay home this year instead of traveling.

Gerry finally told his parents what happened with

the cockroaches, and now the entire family is prepared to face the firing squad. Mom and Pop Guldstein sighed in relief when they found out the next-door neighbors weren't drug addicts or alcoholics. In fact, they even laughed that they could have such an idea in the first place.

"See, I told you to mind your own business," Gerry says. "I've told her over and over again to stop eavesdropping!"

"You always have to add your own two cents," Grandpa tells his wife.

"And you, what about your two cents?" Nana snaps back.

Hannah bangs her feet against her chair to let her opinion be known.

"Okay, you two, let's have a good day," Gerry says to prevent the conversation from escalating into a battle.

Apprehension fills the room as they sit around the kitchen table, staring at one another, trying to decide on a time to go over to the Wilkersens. Roger chases his tail, and then settles at Grandpa's feet. Meanwhile, Hannah sits in her high chair, waving her spoon in the air to get her mother's attention. Grandpa plays a game with Roger, tossing him morsels of scrambled eggs left over from breakfast, and Roger plays a game of his own, bringing the pieces of egg over to Hannah to eat. Gerry gently removes a packing label stuck to his fur near his tail. It is just another reminder of what they brought to their new neighborhood from Manhattan. Stephanie laughs nervously, as does the whole family. Nana changes Roger's scarf to the one she knitted with pockets for cookies to bring next door to Murphy whenever they muster enough nerve to go there.

Back at the Wilkersens', Uncle Bob is cleaning the dishes up with Aunt Tilly's help—an unusual sight under any circumstances. Uncle Arnold takes a photo of this scene as his own Christmas gift to himself. He is ecstatic. Jennifer's camera is glued to her fingers. She is anxious to take photos to share this special Christmas memory with her future children and tell them the story of Christmas with the cockroaches.

The house is almost back to normal, except for the broken items, which Emma says won't be replaced. There are scratches that mar the floor here and there. At any other time Emma would be infuriated. Now she is nonchalant, almost as if she didn't care about her possessions anymore. Jennifer asks her mom how many Valium she has taken, since she is so relaxed.

"Yes dear, I did take one earlier in the morning. I do remember that."

"Are you sure, Mom?"

"Yes, yes, of course I am."

Uncle Bob notes the change in his sister. This is a positive change, back to the way she used to be when she was younger.

In the kitchen, the family makes sure there isn't any food in sight on any of the counters, not even a crumb to attract the cockroaches until the house is sprayed. Murphy and Pookie did a thorough job eating whatever fell on the floor, cleaning it better than a mop.

This Christmas is out of the ordinary in so many ways, and there is one thing, one very significant thing that never happened before—EVERYONE IS STICKING TOGETHER!

Yes, this is a special family occasion after all. Instead of having petty arguments and feelings of jealousy, they worked together as a group to get rid of the Christmas cockroaches. *An unpleasant group of bugs brought fun to this otherwise snobby, plastic, and routine Christmas party,* Uncle Bob thinks. *This should happen every year, but without the roaches!*

Even Theo Jr. and Jennifer help their parents rather than texting or using any of their electronics. Theo Sr. and Emma discovered who their real friends are. Theo Jr. refuses to indulge his girlfriend and decides never to call her back. Jennifer realizes how petty her girlfriends are, that is, except for one whom she intends to keep as a friend. The rest of the family has joined together, and feel more alive.

Aunt Mary and Aunt Tilly believe this was by far their best Christmas with the family, and they are comfortable enough to tell each other so. Aunt Tilly picked up Pookie to hug her, and then Jennifer gave the dogs a bath with Theo Jr.'s help. Even Aunt Tilly, once known for her cooking talents, let her hair down. "I'll volunteer to be chef later on," said Aunt Tilly, "even though it will ruin my beautifully manicured pink nails."

"Just in case you can use this." Emma said, handing her nail polish remover.

For the first time in decades, Emma is not interested in looking at herself in the mirror, though her hives disappeared overnight. Dressed in Theo Sr.'s sweats, she is wiping her own floors with a rag and Murphy's Oil Soap, kneeling down on all fours like her cleaning woman.

After watching Emma, her cheering section of one—her husband—says, "I want you on all fours every day, dear. The floors need you." Theo Sr. feels badly and kneels down on the floor with her, cleaning together the way they did years ago when first married. "Boy, does this ever bring back good memories, Emma. Remember how we used to do this together all the time when we first wed?"

Emma grins back at him, leans her shoulder up against his, and nudges him ever so slightly.

This morning is a learning experience for the Wilkersens, or could be called an etiquette class for the arrogant. The moment is all that matters.

When they gather in the kitchen to eat Uncle Bob's breakfast, they appreciate his efforts.

"Uncle Bob, you are the best cook. This is so yummy!" Jennifer is really enjoying the home cooked meal.

Emma praises the cook with, "I had forgotten what a fabulous chef you are. Thank you for doing this for all of us."

The entire family consumes it gratefully, with no fuss or worry about restricting their intake because of their diets. Everyone wants a second helping. Theo Jr. and Jennifer take thirds.

Their attitudes have changed because of the cockroaches! They laugh with one another. In fact, all that can be heard from the Wilkersens' kitchen is laughter and boisterous conversation.

Sometimes there is silence, a moment for thought, and at those times the family sits around the table smiling at each other eye-to-eye, seeing their real selves, and liking them for who they are.

Uncle Bob announces that he intends to buy a picture frame in which he will put a cockroach, with the date, to commemorate this year's Christmas with the cockroaches.

"That sounds wonderful Bob. I just have one request, and that is that the cockroach not be a live one please." Emma gives her brother an adoring smile like she used to do when they were small children. More laughter fills the room.

Standing at the head of the table, Theo Sr. makes a short speech that ends thus: "Wherever these creatures came from, they have been the greatest gift we could have received. A toast is in order..." He raises his glass of orange juice. Everyone stands and applauds. "Hail, hail to the cockroaches! Hail, hail! Hail, hail to the true holiday spirit!"

Little do the Guldsteins know they are the heroes of the day after all! A new life is beginning for Gerry, Stephanie, Hannah and Roger in their beautiful new home. But past experience still makes Steph worry about the cockroaches that may lurk behind its walls.

At night she roams with her flashlight gleaming, ready to catch sight of a bug creeping along the floor, scurrying across the furniture or infesting her cabinets… And, silently, Gerry wonders too.

Happy Hanukkah and Merry Christmas from the Guldsteins and Wilkersens!

And a very happy holiday to all from the cockroaches!
(Ha-ha)

EPILOGUE

Oh, and by the way... Uncle Bob says that if there is another party like this one, he will be sure to attend!

Pookie is just a poodle now—no more pink fluff! This will save Aunt Tilly's marriage, without a doubt.

Murphy is a happier dog, now that Theo Sr. takes him for longer walks and allows him to ride in their prestigious cars.

Theo Sr.'s western trip was a success, and Emma enjoyed her week of relaxation. Now she wears only lipstick, she says, to keep her lips moist—no more face-fillers.

Jennifer and Theo Jr. feel more connected to their parents since Christmas, and are happy to join them wherever and whenever they wish to go.

And what happened to the Guldsteins? No one

has seen them since the party. They could be hibernating, too tired from their move to go out, or, possibly, they are still hiding from their neighbors, afraid to admit their responsibility for bringing the cockroaches with them. Perhaps they've discovered some uninvited guests of their own... Only time will tell.

ABOUT THE AUTHOR

Libbe Leah always carried pens and a journal with her as a child, and now as an author working full-time at her craft, her many notebooks are full of memorable characters in the most unusual situations, such as *"Christmas with the Cockroaches."*

Her numerous interests have assumed secondary roles to her true passion of writing. She has self-published five books for young children: *Hummer Bummer Bee Has Lost his Buzz, Vol.1; Hummer Marries Zzub, Vol.2; Please Don't Pick the Pansies; Farmer Dueey Dew and Cabbage Rabbit Too*; and *Mae's Vacuum*. She also has several stories in the works, including a fantasy trilogy for children and young adults, *The Kingdom of Irisia,* and a compelling novel, *The Story of Haggy Baggy*, about a young girl's sudden disappearance and the effect on her family.

A Thorn in Rose's Garden, the unedited story of Libbe's life as a child in the care of her abusive stepmother, was self-published in 2011. One reader commented, "The author tells it like she lived it…much of it will be very hard to read, and yet hard to stop reading at the same time." She is now working on a memoir that encompasses not only that time in her life, but also all that followed.

Libbe lives in Boston, where she was born and raised.